Beyond This Bitter Air

ILLINOIS SHORT FICTION

A list of books in the series appears at the end of this volume.

Sarah Rossiter

Beyond This Bitter Air

UNIVERSITY OF ILLINOIS PRESS

Urbana and Chicago

Publication of this work was supported in part
by grants from the Illinois Arts Council, a state agency,
and the National Endowment for the Arts.

© 1987 by Sarah Rossiter
Manufactured in the United States of America
C 5 4 3 2 1

This book is printed on acid-free paper.

"Tea Party," *Ontario Review* (Winter 1981–82): *The Way We Live Now*
   (anthology), Ontario Review Press, 1986.
"Kiss the Father," *Massachusetts Review* (Spring 1985).
"Pandora," *Ontario Review* (Spring 1984).
"Sinners," *North American Review* (September 1983).
"Civil War," *North American Review* (forthcoming, 1987).

Library of Congress Cataloging-in-Publication Data

Rossiter, Sarah.
   Beyond this bitter air.

   (Illinois short fiction)
   Contents: Combinations—Star light, star bright—Tea party—[etc.]
   I. Title. II. Series.
PS3568.08477B4 1987   813'.54   87–5031
ISBN 0–252–01429–4 (alk. paper)

For Ned

I cry to you beyond upon this bitter air.
        —Archibald MacLeish, "Immortal Autumn"

Contents

Combinations   1

Star Light, Star Bright   14

Tea Party   25

Kiss the Father   40

Question of Light   48

Sinners   58

Skinner   73

Secrets   84

Pandora   99

Civil War   115

Combinations

Because it's a six-hour drive we leave early in the morning. Concord is quiet, the streets shaded by large trees whose leaves have already begun to turn. Lawns are still green, but the roadside grass is stiff and brown.

"I used to like fall," I say.

Ian is driving. Instead of answering, he starts to tap his fingers against the wheel. I listen to the rhythm, hoping to decipher the tune in his head. After a few minutes I give up.

Rolling down the window, I start to sing "There Is a Green Hill Far Away." The solemn beat is soothing, but the resonance is missing. The hymn drifts, small and sad, out the window, back into the car.

"Christ, Ma!"

Ian switches on the radio, and I am drowned out by Stevie Wonder.

"You used to like hymns," I say.

There is no answer.

Once on the turnpike the rush of air feels good. It smells good too, ripe grapes and burning leaves. Although the sun is barely up, it's already warm, more August than September.

"It's going to be a scorcher," I say.

Ian grunts.

The wind blows across me, and I tuck my hands beneath the sweater in my lap. The sweater is hardly necessary but its small weight gives comfort. I remember when Ian was very small, and every afternoon we'd nap together on the big bed, Frank's and mine, with the door closed and the curtains drawn. I remember how the room was cool and quiet, and how he lay on me, his head tucked just beneath my chin. He was so light, the weight of feathers. I remember the sound of our breathing as we drifted into sleep.

I glance at him, see the wind blowing his fine straight hair off his forehead, revealing white skin untouched by summer sun. And I feel strangely guilty, as if looking at something too private to be seen.

His first year, Ian was completely bald. "His head," friends said, sensing my unspoken terror. "What a marvelous shape!" It wasn't the lack of hair that had me terrified but the prolonged exposure of that soft spot beating so gently on the top of his head. For twelve months I was confronted by that fragile pulse. Cradling him I scarcely dared breathe for fear of puncturing such tenuous skin. The others were born with masses of dark curls, and I learned, slowly, not to worry. But Ian was first; and my fear has stayed with me.

Harriet comes on the radio, her nasal voice summoning women to what she calls "the biggest event of your lives, a cosmetic sale with prices so low that. . . ." Ian and I reach for the knob at the same time. Our fingers touch. I pull back quickly.

Ian is seventeen. Until last year I kissed him good night. Every night. Until last year he would be lying in bed, his door open, waiting, and I would smooth his hair back from his forehead and kiss his cheek. Now his door is closed, and if I go in he's always standing, always dressed. "What do you want?" he says. To kiss him I have to stand up on my tiptoes. He is two inches taller than Frank, eight inches taller than me. It is like climbing a ladder to reach his cheek. Lately I've been shouting "Good night" through the closed door. "Night," he calls back. Sometimes.

"I can't believe we're doing this," I say when another song ends. Ever since we planned this trip I've been storing up things to say, things to talk about. All I need is an opening. "Yeah," says Ian. I decide to wait; it's a long trip. There's lots of time.

Ian learned to talk when he was very young. We were living in England then, and when I think of England I think of Ian perched on the flowered sofa, legs straight out, hands folded in his lap. His head was covered with peach fuzz, and his eyes enormous, round and blue. He was eighteen months old, and I was sitting beside him, drinking tea when he looked at me, and said, "Let's talk about the combinations." I was so surprised I almost choked. "Goodness," I said when I could talk. "Where did you learn that fancy word?" And Ian smiled. He was so pleased. "Combinations," he said again. He said it often after that, whenever he wanted to have what he came to call a "conversation."

I try to remember those conversations, but I can't.

Last month Frank came into the kitchen where I was washing dishes. He'd been weeding in the garden, and his hands were filthy. I moved aside to let him use the sink. "Lucy," he said, "I think it would be better if you took Ian to see that place." I watched his square hands turn the soap until just the right amount of lather was acquired, watched the careful spreading of his fingers. I knew what place he meant.

Frank is an economist. The day his thesis was accepted, Ian was born. Frank bought two bottles of champagne to celebrate what he called a "felicitous combination of events." As a nursing mother I was allowed only one small glass. Frank, who drank the rest, danced around my bed with a pillowcase on his head while I begged him to stop because it hurt to laugh. It's the only time in twenty years I've seen him have too much to drink.

I watched Frank rinse his hands and dry them carefully, first making sure the towel was clean. "Why me?" I said. He took his glasses off to clean them. "Because," he said. And that was that.

A private consultant, Frank has his office in the house, which means that I've spent years training children into silence. As there are six, it hasn't been easy, for them or me. "Did you notice how quiet the kids were today?" I used to say to Frank at dinner. He'd blink at me above his glasses. "Can't say that I did."

I notice, now, that Ian's doing seventy. I also know there're speed traps on this road. One day not long ago I was stopped three times in sixty miles. "Jesus, lady," the third cop said. "You're getting something of a reputation."

"Long-distance driving," I said. "I go into some kind of trance."

"Yeah," said the cop. "That happens to me too."

A nice man. He smiled, writing out the ticket.

Frank didn't smile when I placed three tickets on his desk. "What's this?" he said. His mouth was thin. "A little fame," I said, thinking maybe I could make him laugh. He closed his eyes. "Lucy," he said.

"What are we going to do with you?"

The speedometer hovers at sixty-eight, but I say nothing. The fact is I have been trained in silence too.

Though there are times when I forget, like last month when I walked into Ian's room, I can't remember now for what, but it's a room I seldom enter anymore, and what first struck me was the smell. Stench is more apt, the stench of socks and sweat, rotting apples and sour milk. Because of the black lights he uses, I couldn't see too well, but as my eyes adjusted I saw that every surface was covered, with clothes and paintings. Records. Books. His sheets looked gray. He stood there, in the middle of the room, before his easel. He didn't look at me. I took a step toward him, and I tripped on something and stubbed my toe. It was surprising how much it hurt, and I forgot my vow of silence, my resolution not to nag. Forgetting, I began to shout. I'm afraid I can't remember what I said. Ian, I know, said nothing, but stood, his head bent, his face like bone in the unnatural light. It was his silence that finally silenced me. "I'm sorry," I said, as if the fault were mine.

My mother tells me that as a child I never stopped: my talking drove her crazy is what she says. I was nine when I discovered writing, discovered that on paper I could say whatever I wanted, and no one would tell me to go away. "I'm going to be a writer," I said proudly to my mother, who was weeding in the garden. "Lucy," she said, "you're on my parsley. Step back please."

When our youngest child started school, I said to Frank I wanted a study of my own. "If you think it will help," Frank said, voice trailing off. But he's a practical man with competent hands. He took a large closet, and put in a skylight and soundproofed the walls. The walls were white, the desk was brown. There was nothing to look at. I left the door open. It didn't help. I heard the silence. "I can't work there," I said. I heard Frank sigh.

"I can't," I said to Ian, who was fifteen. He pressed his fingertips against the closet walls. "You're right," he said. "Bad vibes." He smiled at me. "You can use my room when I'm gone."

I glance at his hands resting loosely on the wheel. There's dirt beneath the nails, but his fingers, unlike his father's, are long and thin. The fingers of an artist. He sees me looking. He frowns. "I know," he says. "They're dirty."

"That's not what I was thinking!" I say. "Don't be so sensitive. You have beautiful hands."

"Jesus!" He curls his fingers tight around the wheel. I look away.

His fingers were the second thing I noticed when he was born. The first was his umbilical cord, which I mistook for his penis. Because he was the first, I was still hazy about the appropriate size of things. He was born in England, at home, a midwife in attendance. "Ian, is it?" she said. "A lovely name."

"Lucy," said Frank. "In six months we'll be gone from here. He'll have that name for the rest of his life."

"And look at his fingers," Nurse Salmon said. "Aren't they lovely too!"

They were. Long and thin with small pink nails like tiny shells. Nursing, he'd knead my breasts, gently, the way a kitten does. I spent hours nursing him because being a novice I was unsure how much he needed, and because when he wasn't nursing he was crying. I never knew a baby could cry so much and still survive. There were times when I thought I might not survive as well. Frank, who was teaching then, spent days and sometimes nights at school. I didn't mind; it meant I didn't have to worry about him too.

I glance at my watch. We've been driving for two hours, and we haven't talked at all. "Do you know," I say, smiling, "as a baby you cried more than all the others put together."

"I know," he says. "You've told me that before." His voice is flat. His eyes are on the road.

"You were hypersensitive," I say. "That's what the doctor said."

Ian says nothing. Leaning forward, his chin rests on the steering wheel. I can't see his face. I hear Elvis singing "Don't Be Cruel." I loved Elvis when I was Ian's age. Ian's always hated him. When he doesn't turn it off, I do.

"He said that hypersensitive babies almost always turn into creative people. Did I tell you that?"

"A hundred times." His voice is patient, resigned. He sounds much older than he is. I wonder how many conversations we've had I can't remember. I wonder, if I dared to lay my hand on the top of his head would I still feel that gentle throbbing?

He was four when he began to draw. He drew all day. At nursery school his paintings were always on the wall, complex colorful designs, and in them I saw dragons, monsters, a winged horse. "A visionary," I said to Frank. Frank took a drawing in his strong clean hands. He looked at it. He shook his head. "*You're* the visionary," he said.

Two more children had been born by then, but when I had the time I'd write stories for the drawings, and even sent them off. They all came back.

"Ian," I ask, "do you still have your early drawings?"

"You're kidding," says Ian. "I threw that junk out years ago."

At the next tollbooth we change places. Ian leans toward the radio. "Don't," I say. "Let's talk."

Ian slumps back and closes his eyes. I pretend I haven't noticed.

"Can you believe next year you'll be away at college?"

There is no answer. I try again.

"Are you excited?"

"What?" he mumbles.

"About art school?"

Eyes closed, he shrugs. "I haven't seen it yet."

It's the kind of remark his father would make. I let it pass, though what I want to say is that if it weren't for me he'd be looking at Princeton, not art school. I don't say it. I suspect he knows this anyway.

"It's what he wants," I said to Frank not long ago. Frank took his glasses off to look at me. I've noticed recently he does this whenever I try to talk to him. Without his glasses, he can't see a thing. "Did he say so?" Frank asked. It was night, and we were both in bed. Frank held the *Wall Street Journal* on his lap.

"He doesn't have to say. I know!"

Frank blinked, peering at me as if trying to remember who I was.

"Let's leave it to the boy," he said.

"He's hardly a boy!"

Frank slipped his glasses into place. "I don't know what else he is." He bent above the paper again.

In the car the rearview mirror is tilted at such an angle that I can look at Ian without being observed. Anyway, his eyes are closed, and I think maybe he's asleep. In silence I study his face. It has a sharpness now that wasn't there a year ago. His mouth is firm, no longer soft. It's like looking at a stranger, and yet there are still traces, in the arch of eyebrows, the curve of chin, of who he was.

Last week I took some early photographs from a drawer, and spent the morning going through them. There is one especially I've always liked, a picture of his legs when he was three. We were back from England then but he looks very English anyway in plaid shorts and small red sandals. Very English his legs seem too, rosy and plump, blond hairs glinting in the sun. I spent the morning studying that picture, trying to connect those legs to the long bony legs I glimpse occasionally as he sprints into the bathroom. But there was no connection, none at all, and only the fly perched on the rounded knee seemed real.

"He's not going to be an economist, you know," I said that night to Frank in bed.

"The last thing I expect," said Frank. He turned his page.

"You just want him to go to Princeton because you did."

"Lucy," said Frank. "How do you know that's what I want?"

"Because we've been married twenty years."

Frank lowered the paper. He took off his glasses and rubbed his eyes. "Have we really?" He sounded surprised.

We have. And in December I'll be forty, which means I've been married for half my life.

"You ought to know," I said to Frank.

Frank sighed. "You can't expect me to remember things like that."

I wondered. After twenty years what is it I expect?

In June the sugar maple that's shaded our house for a hundred years succumbed to some mysterious blight. Within a month the leaves yellowed, withered, dropped. By July the tree was bare.

I wondered if I should take it as a sign.

"I'm almost forty," I said to a good friend the other day, "and what have I done?"

"You're the mother of men," my good friend said.

I wasn't looking at her so I didn't see that she was smiling.

"What about the girls?" I said.

"For heaven's sake," she said. "I'm joking!" When I looked at her she shook her head. A gentle shake. "What's happened to your sense of humor?"

I glance into the mirror again, looking not at Ian but myself. The frown lines across my forehead are definitely more pronounced. She's right. I don't laugh often anymore.

When Ian was small, I only had to look at him to laugh. We had a private language then. "Let's talk about the combinations," he'd say, sitting in my lap, and we'd rock together in our yellow chair. "There are all kinds of combinations," I'd say to him. "For instance . . ." I whispered in his ear, "underwear." When he laughed, I'd laugh too. "Oh Ian," I'd say, "Ian!"

When he was small, he frightened easily. Going to the doctor's was the worst. He hated it. I'd sit beside him, one hand on his forehead, the other on his leg. He clutched my arm. I stroked his skin. "It's all right, love. Mummy's here." The doctor cleared his throat, chair creaking as he swiveled back and forth. "Perhaps," he said, "it's time to think of having the next." His tone was kind, but I knew what he was really saying.

I wonder, sometimes, if I had so many just to prove him wrong.

I love the children. In a way each is a poem I never wrote. I did write though; at least I tried. When they were small I wrote standing at the kitchen counter so none of them could climb into my lap. I wrote poems, and when I had enough I typed them neatly and sent them off. In two weeks they were back, four years of work, and the strand of hair I'd placed in the middle was still in place.

"They came back," I said to Frank who took his glasses off, and sighed. "What?" he said. He rubbed his eyes.

"They came back," I said to Ian who was nine. Ian knew exactly what I meant. One eye was covered by his shaggy hair; the other eye was round and wise. It looked at me. "If at first you don't succeed," said Ian, "try and try again." I pushed the hair back from his eye. "What would I do without you?" I kissed his nose. He pulled away. "There're plenty more where I came from," he said, and sprinted quickly out the door.

I look at him, his eyes still closed. The car is hot, and I am sticky. Hungry too. I'm glad of the plans I've made for lunch, plans I've kept from Ian because I know that he'd object. But I don't care. There's so much to say, so little time.

"I don't see why we couldn't stop at Burger King?" Ian says. His voice is sullen. He rolls a bit of bread between his fingers. The bread is gray.

Determined not to ruin things by telling him to wash his hands, I look away, around the restaurant. It's cool and quiet, dimly lit. The air smells sweet. Though twenty years have passed, I can't see that much has changed. The same checked tablecloths, and on each table one small pink rose, a bud, the petals tightly closed.

"I used to come here with your father."

I watch Ian pulling at the bread.

"Why do you always call him that?" he says.

"Because that's what he is."

"It sounds so stupid."

I sigh, wishing the waiter would appear so I can order a drink. Normally I don't like to drink at lunch because after drinking all I crave is sleep. Today is different, and anyway his interview isn't till tomorrow.

"Okay," I say. "How about 'I used to come here with my husband'?"

I'm rewarded with a grin.

"That's even worse," he says.

"Monsieur et Madame!"

A white-coated waiter hovers above our table. When I look at him, he winks at me.

"An aperitif, perhaps?"

He hands a wine list to Ian, and disappears. Ian and I exchange a look.

"Hey," says Ian, grinning. "How old does he think I am!"

He looks so pleased I have to smile.

"How about me?" I say. "Did you see him winking?"

"Maybe he's like Dad," says Ian. "He can't see without his glasses."

"Thanks a lot," I say, and Ian laughs. I lean toward him. "I have the feeling he thinks we're up to something."

"Mom!" Ian shouts with laughter.

"Shh," I say, smiling. "Don't ruin his fun."

I persuade Ian to try sangría. "It's like fruit punch," I say. "Remember how you used to like that Kool-Aid kind?"

"No," says Ian, but he smiles, and after taking a sip, he nods. "It's okay," he says, "but I'd rather have St. Pauli Girl."

On his sixteenth birthday we offered him a beer. "The place to learn to drink is home," I said, proud of our progressive ways.

"What's to learn?" said Ian. "And anyway I only like St. Pauli Girl. The other stuff all tastes like piss."

As I never bought St. Pauli Girl, I've never seen him drink. I see him now. He's gulping down sangría as if it's Kool-Aid. I'd say something except I notice I've been gulping too. Grinning, he refills our glasses.

I lean back, and light a cigarette. I don't know when I've felt so happy. I smile at him.

"Let's talk about the combinations," I say.

He stares at me, his hair falling across one eye. I long to push it back.

"Are you already drunk?" he says.

"Don't you remember! You used to say that all the time."

"I did not!"

He says this so emphatically that for an instant I wonder if he's right.

I shake my head. "Isn't it funny how people always remember different things?"

He turns his wine glass back and forth. "Yeah," he says. His voice is sad and far away.

The waiter returns, flourishing his pen. He looks very French, with a droopy mustache and a rose in his lapel. He leers at me while asking Ian if we're ready to order. Does he think I'm one of those women with a penchant for younger men? Or is it possible in this dim light that he truly thinks we're close in age?

It might be possible I guess.

Last month Frank found me in the living room, standing on the sofa. Our youngest was beside me. He watched us leaping to a nearby chair.

"That's swamp," I said, pointing at the floor. "Alligators and things like that."

"Lucy," said Frank, in the same tone the pediatrician had used so many years before. A gentle warning.

I wonder sometimes if having so many children has prevented me from growing up.

"Monsieur?" Pen poised, the waiter waits impatiently. Ian looks at me, beseeching, and I realize the menu is in French; Ian has had six years of Spanish.

"I'll go first," I say. "Crêpes des champignons, and a salad."

"Me too," says Ian, who only wants to get the ordering over before his age and ignorance are revealed. I'm careful not to smile, but I do order more sangría and request more bread so he won't leave the table starving. He has always hated mushrooms.

I'm sure that as soon as the waiter leaves, he'll start complaining, but instead he cocks his head and leans toward me.

"This place is okay," he says.

"We came here all the time," I say, concealing my surprise. "What's amazing is that it hasn't changed at all."

Hunching forward, he studies my face with an air of concentration. In his painting it's the intensity I admire most, but now, directed at me, I am uncomfortable. I look down at the table.

"I just can't see it," Ian says. "I just can't see the two of you making it, if you know what I mean."

I don't know what he means. Is he talking about marriage? Sex? Head down, I blush.

"It was a long time ago," I say, hedging. "One night we were here five hours, discussing tragedy. They finally had to kick us out."

"I don't believe it," Ian says.

"It's true."

"I mean, I can't imagine it. You guys talking. Like that."

When I look up, he shakes his head.

"Actually," I say, softly, "I can't either."

He's still staring. Under such scrutiny, I feel exposed. It's the way Frank stared when we first met.

"You made a mistake," says Ian.

I pleat my napkin like a fan, fingering the folds.

"Ian," I say. "I would never have had you."

"Not that," says Ian. "Not getting married. A mistake to have so many kids."

I look surprised. "But I wanted them, Ian."

He looks away.

"Why?" he says.

Why. Why is it that no one has ever asked before. Even Frank has accepted what he calls my "perpetual obsession," though he did ask if the last child was really necessary. "Frank," I said, before I thought, "without the children what would we have to talk about?" As I recall, he didn't answer.

"It's complicated," I say to Ian. "A combination, really."

I'm saved by the arrival of the crêpes. Again I wait for Ian to complain. Again he smiles. "Good," he mumbles, his mouth full.

"You have grown up! Remember how you hated mushrooms?"

"We're still talking about you," he says. He looks at me. "If you hadn't had so many you could have done more with your writing."

"There's still time," I say. "Maybe."

Ian says nothing. He looks at me.

"Anyway." I shrug. "I'm just not good enough."

"Bullshit!" says Ian with great force. "You were just too scared to really try!"

His vehemence surprises me. It scares me too.

"Don't talk with your mouth full."

His eyes are fierce. "You can't get rid of me that easily," he says.

I look at him, and think of next year when he'll be gone. My throat goes tight.

"Oh, Ian," I say. "I don't want to get rid of you at all."

He blinks. I lean toward him.

"You're the only one who understands."

He doesn't answer. He doesn't need to.

I smile. "Remember the Quiet Game?" I say.

"No," says Ian.

But I remember, remember how when he was small, he liked to press his nose to mine and we would stare unblinking into each other's eyes until in silence a secret bond was formed.

It's what I feel now. An understanding without words.

For dessert we order mousse. I hold the chocolate on my tongue, and, savoring, let hot coffee slide around it. I need the coffee after all that wine. I sit, sleepy, watching Ian gulp his mousse and order more.

The waiter brings another. I ask for coffee. When I thank him, he nods curtly. Now that he's realized what we are, he finds us boring. Without a glance at Ian, he hands the check to me.

I sit, sipping coffee, watching Ian eat. He leans over, taking slow careful bites as if afraid he'll still be hungry when he's done.

"When you were a baby," I say, "I was always afraid you weren't getting enough to eat."

"Don't tell me," Ian says. He's so hunched over that all I see is the top of his head.

"It was your crying," I say. "And your soft spot. I was really terrified to hold you."

Ian pushes his mousse away, and sits up straight.

"I'm sick of hearing that stuff!" he says. "I mean, how many times do you have to tell me what a crappy baby I was?"

His voice is loud. I stare at him.

"Ian! That's not what I've been saying at all."

"Bullshit it isn't. All my life, that's all you've ever said." He leans toward me. His face is close. His eyes are angry. "How come you never talk about the others that way?"

"The others are different."

"Yeah." He laughs, a harsh, sad sound. "I know." He slumps back, away from me, and stares into his empty glass. "I mean, if at first you don't succeed, try and try again." He looks at me. "That's why you had so many, isn't it?"

I sit there, stunned.

"Ian," I say slowly. "Nothing, absolutely nothing, could be further from the truth."

"Truth," says Ian. He laughs again, the same harsh sound, and shrugs. "The truth is you never cared for me at all."

All I can do is stare at him.

"I can't believe it," I say. "I can't believe you never knew."

Star Light, Star Bright

Lucy stands in the hall outside her grandmother's apartment. When she hears the elevator descending, she kneels, quickly, and touches her forehead to the doorknob. She feels cold metal burn her skin. She smells Brasso, sees the green twisting vines, faded now, climbing the walls, sees the ceiling disappear above her head. Kneeling, she remembers how small the world was when she was five. How large.

She has to stand to reach the doorbell.

Lucy is twenty-nine. She stands, listening to the bell ring through the wall, wishing, now, she hadn't come.

This winter Lucy has been waking in the night. She lies in bed, staring at the ceiling. Justin sleeps beside her. They have been married for three years, and he sleeps soundly, his breathing steady, in and out. The room is cold. Justin prefers the windows open. The shades are down. The stars are hidden by the ceiling, perhaps by clouds as well, but lying there, Lucy sees them anyway, sees them as she saw them as a child, bright pricks of light fixed against a velvet sky.

At least she tries to, but she is twenty-nine, and last month Justin told her that the universe is expanding.

Think of raisins in a pudding, he said, the raisins as stars. When the pudding rises, the raisins move apart. Infinite expansion, said Justin, smiling.

Now at night she lies awake and thinks, not of the stars but of the space between them.

She thinks of Honey in Chicago.

"I want to see her," Lucy said.

Justin closed one eye, as if peering through his telescope.

"Why?"

Sitting at the kitchen table, peering, not at Lucy but at the wall above her head. As if trying to measure distance. Did he really want to know? Lucy wasn't sure that she could tell him. She put the box of Bran Flakes on the table.

"She meant a lot to me," said Lucy, and then she blushed. In her family no one ever mentioned feelings. "I lived with her," said Lucy. "You know that. When I was little. For a while she and Olga were all I had."

Justin shook his cereal into his bowl. Lucy watched, saw his hand gripping the box, shaking, knowing exactly when to stop.

"She made me feel safe," said Lucy.

Justin looked at Lucy. His eyes were blue, cloudless as a summer day. "Lucy," he said, "what will it prove? What is the point? If she can't recognize anyone anymore?"

"It's only family she can't recognize," said Lucy.

Justin smiled, and Lucy saw the space between his teeth.

"But what are you?"

This winter, at the bookstore where she works, Lucy hung a set of wind chimes from the ceiling. When the door opened, the chimes began to ring, a silver sound reminding her of Honey, of Honey's bell, the one she rang to summon Olga. Thinking of Honey, Lucy began to cry.

Steve, the owner, put down his book. Embarrassed, Lucy wiped her eyes.

"I don't know what's wrong with me."

"A perfect Pisces," Steve said, explaining Lucy to herself.

She closed her eyes. "Did you know the universe is expanding?"

"Not everyone thinks so."

"Do you?"

"It's expanding now," said Steve. "But no one knows how much density there is up there. Like hidden weight. If there's enough, there'll be enough gravity to pull us, it, back together again. Eventually."

"What do you think?" Lucy asked.

"I think there's plenty."

"I hope you're right," said Lucy.

"Listen," said Steve. "I'll do your chart."

"That won't help," said Lucy. "The problem's not out there." She touched her heart. "It's here."

"For that," said Steve, "you go back. Find the Source."

What source? Lucy didn't ask.

Instead she goes to visit Honey.

She calls her cousins, thinking they might want to come, but when they don't, she's secretly relieved. "What kind of trip is that?" said Rob, who during college dealt in drugs. Not trip, thinks Lucy. Mission. Honey has somehow slipped away. It's up to Lucy to bring her back.

Olga opens the door. "It's you," she says in her flat voice. There's no surprise. She looks at Lucy. Her eyes, magnified by steel-rimmed glasses, are pale blue. Her hair is white. Her face reminds Lucy of a snow-covered field. Olga, the family says, is ninety-three.

She holds the door, and Lucy steps inside. On the surface nothing's changed. She smells lavender and dust. Bookshelves line the wall: old books, mostly history. Decline and Fall. The air is hot, and the walls so thick that no sound penetrates from the city streets.

"My parents called you, didn't they?" says Lucy. "To tell you I was coming?"

Olga reaches past her to close the door. Her arms are whiter than her uniform. Under the skin blue veins rise like rope. Lucy hears the locks click into place.

"You're here," she says, but there's no telling if she thinks that's good or bad.

Olga has been here all Lucy's life. Whenever Lucy thinks of Honey, she thinks of Olga too. Like Honey, Olga simply is, has always been.

Lucy looks around. On the hall table she sees the blue bowl filled with paper-whites in bloom. She sees the family photographs are gone.

"Where is she?" Lucy says, afraid she'll see her, afraid she won't.

"Where do you think?" says Olga.

Lucy doesn't know. The flowers look like small white stars. She leans toward them. All her life she's wished on stars. Bending, Lucy breathes deep, smelling sweetness, smelling spring. Her eyes water. She wants to cry.

"How is she?" she asks Olga, who takes her coat. When Olga opens the closet door Lucy sees Honey's fur coat gleaming through a plastic bag. She smells the mothballs, remembering when Honey went out every single day.

Olga's crepe-soled shoes are soundless on the parquet floor. No sound comes from anywhere. Olga reaches out, surprising Lucy. Reaching out, she touches Lucy's hand.

"You'll see," she says.

What Lucy sees is Honey, sitting in her chair, in the living room by the unlit fire, and for a moment she thinks, why, nothing's changed. Smaller maybe, but that's all. Honey has a blue shawl across her shoulders, and a yellow blanket on her lap. She stares straight ahead, out the window at gray winter sky.

"Mrs. Knight?" says Olga softly, and Honey turns.

She turns, and looks at Lucy. Her eyes narrow in her small fierce face. "Get out!" she says. "I won't have strangers in my house!" Lucy knows the face, the sharp jaw and beaky nose, but not the voice. A high voice, full of fear, of feeling. Lucy feels her legs begin to shake.

"It's me," she says. "It's Lucy."

Thinking of once, long ago, when she was just a child, and her father, his guard down, said, "You're Honey's favorite," forgetting that in their family no one said such things. Then, maybe, he remembered. "Not favorite," he said. "She doesn't believe in favorites. But you're the one she knows the best."

"Lucy," Lucy says again to Honey. "Your granddaughter. Lucy."

Honey straightens. Her eyes flash. Beneath the yellow blanket her hands rise, forming fists.

"How dare you!" she says. "I never married. I have never had a family!"

"Never mind," says Olga.

Lucy sits at the kitchen table, trying not to cry. She bites her lip. The kitchen smells of gingerbread. She wonders if Honey is doing it on purpose, and feels ashamed.

"These things happen," says Lucy, knowing she sounds just like her father.

Olga brings her milk and cookies. "Eat up," she says, the way she used to. Lucy blinks to keep from crying, closes her eyes to drink her milk.

Eyes closed, she hears the kettle humming, and she remembers how it used to be, remembering every day the same routine.

First breakfast with Olga in the kitchen, the kettle steaming, the fresh squeezed juice, and at eight the sound of Honey's bell ringing from the dining room, where it was always Lucy's job to lift the warmer from her toast.

It was Lucy who had named her Honey.

"I'd always thought that someone did that as a joke," said Justin.

"A mistake," said Lucy. "She was spreading honey on her toast and she let me have a bite. It was the first word I ever said."

"Do you remember saying it?" Justin asked.

"No," said Lucy.

But she remembers the smell of coffee and the *New York Times,* of cigarettes, of cold fur coming through the door at noon after Honey's daily walk. Even now, years later, when she hears the noon whistle blow in Cambridge, she thinks of Honey, the sound of ice, the ringing bell, the smell of lunch. And at six, in winter, Lucy thinks of bedtime, thinks of stars.

"I just can't see her being kind to you," said Justin. "Or warm."

"She was though," Lucy said. "In her own way. But mostly she was there. She made an effort. For two years, until my parents came back from the war."

"That's a long time," said Justin.

"She's always been there," Lucy said.

Lucy opens her eyes and sees Olga standing, watching her. She doesn't know what Olga's thinking.

"At least I saw her," Lucy says. "That's what I wanted. It's not that we ever really talked."

She tries to smile. Olga looks at Lucy, blinking.

"There's a way," says Olga in her flat voice, and for a moment Lucy hears it as the Way, imagines low clouds parting, a path of sunlight breaking through.

Lucy shakes her head. "It's okay," she says. "Really."

But Olga walks over to the kitchen closet. The door creaks open. Lucy smells Ajax and ammonia. Olga takes a pale green uniform from a hanger and holds it up to Lucy's shoulders.

"It fits," she says.

"Who's this?" says Honey in her new high voice. Her eyes are bright. Suspicious.

"Dolores," says Olga. "She's come to do your hair."

Lucy steps backward, but Olga is behind her. She nudges Lucy forward. Honey huddles in her chair. Her jaw quivers. "I've never seen her in my life." Her voice quivers too, with fear, or rage.

"That's right," says Olga. "You haven't. She's Patty's first cousin once removed. Patty couldn't come today. She sent Dolores instead."

Can this be Olga? Lying so easily in her calm flat voice. Lucy feels betrayed. She turns to Olga. "You didn't tell me," she says, whispering, so Honey won't hear.

"If I had," says Olga, "you wouldn't have tried it on." She reaches out to straighten Lucy's collar. "There."

"Don't just stand there," Honey says. "Come closer. I want to see your face."

"She's not used to being in uniform," says Olga.

"You told me I was trying it on for Patty!" says Lucy, no longer whispering.

"You are," says Honey. "Come here."

Lucy has no choice. She feels the green dress bunch around her waist as she walks across the room to Honey. She waits for Honey's eyes to widen in shock and fear.

Honey studies her face and nods, a brief bobbing, like a bird.

"There's a resemblance," she says. "Family always shows up in the eyes. But what's wrong with Patty? Patty always comes."

"She took sick," says Olga. "I'll call to find out how she is."

And Olga leaves the room, leaving Lucy there, alone.

"I have to tell you something," says Lucy.

"You don't," says Honey. "I see it for myself. You've no experience, have you?"

"No," says Lucy, "but it's not that."

"I knew it," says Honey. "I knew the minute I laid eyes on you. My eyes are much sharper than people think." She looks at Lucy as if expecting her to disagree.

"I'm sure that's true," says Lucy.

"Speak up," says Honey. "A soft voice doesn't carry very far."

"No," says Lucy. She looks to see if Honey's wearing her hearing aid; of course she isn't. "If I was meant to hear, I'd hear," she used to say.

"Sit down," says Honey. "You make me nervous."

She nods to a footstool by her chair, the same stool Lucy sat on as a child, a blue seat, scratchy, embroidered with green and yellow flowers.

When Lucy sits, her dress rides up. She pulls it down. Her legs are long. She wraps her arms around her knees and looks at Honey, who sits, hands hidden beneath the blanket, sits, not moving. Lucy remembers when her hands were always busy, knitting, sewing, turning the pages of a book. Honey did not believe in wasting time.

"Where's Olga?" Honey says.

"Calling Patty, I guess."

Honey looks down at Lucy.

"Patty *talks* to me," she says.

Lucy blushes. "I don't know what to say."

"She talks," says Honey. "She tells me all about her family."

"You wouldn't want to hear about mine," says Lucy.

"Sometimes," says Honey, "she talks too much." She frowns. "What did you say your name was?"

It takes Lucy a moment to remember. "Dolores, I guess."

"You guess!"

"Dolores."

"Dreadful," says Honey. "Whoever named you that?"

"My family," says Lucy-Dolores. As Dolores, she suddenly feels braver. "What about you?" she says. "Your family?"

"I thought I made that clear." Honey turns to the silver bell, resting on the table beside her. She picks it up and rings it, loud.

She's still ringing when Olga comes, comes so quickly that Lucy knows she's been waiting outside the door.

She carries a towel, a can of dry shampoo, a brush.

"How are you getting on?" she says.

"She's not Patty," says Honey. "But she'll do."

"Good," says Olga. She's careful not to look at Lucy. Placing the things on the table, she leaves.

"Don't just sit there," Honey says. "Get to work."

It occurs to Lucy that, as Dolores, she has nothing left to lose. She stands up, slowly.

"Do you always order people around?"

Honey's forehead wrinkles when she frowns. "What did you say?"

"In my family," says Lucy, "it was important to say please."

"I'm glad," says Honey, "that you were properly brought up." Her lips are tight.

"My grandmother thought good manners were important."

"Did she indeed?" says Honey. But Lucy can tell that she's not listening.

The truth is she was never good at listening, perhaps because she couldn't hear. Or didn't want to. But she would sit, right where she's sitting now, as the family swirled around her, filling the room with family sound. She'd sit, small and erect, more regal presence than a person. An aging ageless presence. Fixed. Unchanging.

"Please," says Honey, primly. "You only need to stand behind me, and drape the towel around my neck."

Lucy stands behind her. The towel is thick and soft and blue. Blue was Honey's favorite color. It smells of soap, and, strangely, sunlight. Honey tucks her head down, and Lucy lays the towel carefully across her shoulders, feeling bone beneath her fingers. Her face burns.

"I don't know what to do," she says.

"Read the instructions," says Honey.

So Lucy does. Out loud.

"Shake can well. Hold can six inches from hair. Lift sections of hair, and spray underside of each section lightly. Fluff. Wait a few minutes. Then brush hair dry."

Honey sniffs. "A child could do it," she says.

Lucy looks down at Honey's hair, soft wisps the color of winter sky. Beneath her hair she sees pink scalp. "I can't," she says.

"There's no such thing as can't," says Honey. Tart. The way she said it when Lucy was a child.

If Lucy can't, Dolores can. Gently she lifts the hair from Honey's neck. Her neck is wrinkled. Her hair is light as feathers, falling. Lucy shakes the can and sprays. White powder glitters.

"You must have had a grandmother," says Lucy.

"I can't remember," says Honey. "*You* talk. Patty talks. She tells me everything. Too much."

"What does she talk about?"

"Her life, naturally. Her family. She's married a perfectly dreadful man."

"In my family no one talks. Not about important things. Like feelings."

"That's how it should be," Honey says.

"But why?" says Lucy.

"I'm too old to answer questions. Too old for everything. The truth is I should be dead."

"Don't say that," says Lucy.

"If it's true," says Honey, "I'll say it."

"I don't know what's true," says Lucy. "What's real. But I used to. At least I thought I did."

"The fact is," says Honey, "people die every day."

"It's the changing," says Lucy. "That's what I hate."

"One makes an effort," Honey says.

"I know that," says Lucy. "But what kind of effort? In what direction?"

"In Eskimo society," says Honey, "old people know enough to take themselves off."

Lucy stops spraying. She looks down at the top of Honey's head, at white powder that gleams like stars.

"Is that why?"

"Why what?" says Honey. "Get on with your job."

Lucy cups her hands to Honey's hair and lifts, lightly, fluffing.

"But what if people love them?" says Lucy. "Like family?"

"I wouldn't know," says Honey. "I never had one."

"I did," says Lucy. "I do. Parents and a husband. Cousins. I have a grandmother."

"Stop fluffing now and brush," says Honey. Her voice is small and cross. A tired child. Her eyes close. Lucy sees her eyelids, thin as paper.

"The directions say we're supposed to wait," says Lucy.

"For what?" says Honey, frowning.

"I don't know," says Lucy.

She doesn't. She looks around the room, the room that was her world as a child. She sees the same green sofa against the wall, the books, the row of windows that let in light.

"When I was little," says Lucy. "I lived with her. My grandmother."

"Brush," says Honey.

Lucy brushes. Honey's head rocks with the strokes. The powder rises in the hot still air.

"In an apartment," says Lucy. "Just like this. High up. Sealed off. For two years it was the only world I knew."

She looks down at Honey. Her eyes are closed, her face is still.

"I'd have supper early, in the kitchen," says Lucy, "and then I'd come into the living room to say good night. She'd be drinking her martini, listening to the radio. To the news." She pauses, thinking. "To Gabriel Heater."

She waits a moment. And Honey nods.

Lucy brushes. Honey's head rocks gently, back and forth.

"She wasn't very comfortable with children. With anyone, I guess, but I didn't know that then. And she always made an effort. We had this ritual. Maybe she started it because she didn't know what else to do. She wasn't like the grandmothers in books; she wasn't cuddly, but the thing is she was always there. I always knew exactly where she'd be, what she'd be doing. Anyway, we'd stand together at the window, and looking up, we'd find a star. I suppose sometimes we didn't. Sometimes we must have cheated. But we always wished. Every night we wished on stars. They had to be secret wishes to come true."

Lucy stops brushing. "Star light, star bright," she says softly, hoping that Honey will say it too. But Honey's eyes are closed; Lucy sees a small pulse throbbing in her neck. "Wish I may, and wish I might."

There is no response from Honey. Lucy puts her brush down on the table.

"I don't know what she wished, but I always wished the same thing. That I'd get a rocking horse, and that Honey, my grandmother, would never die."

Listening, Lucy hears the flutter of Honey's breath. She touches Honey's hair.

"I still wish. Every night. I wish I'd told her that I loved her. While there was time."

She stands behind Honey, looking down. Only the faintest outline of Honey's body shows through layers of blanket, shawl, and towel. She looks so small, so hidden. Standing behind her, Lucy feels very large and very old.

"I'm twenty-nine," she says.

Honey opens her eyes.

"If you're done."

Her hand rises from beneath the blanket. Her fingers are bent. She wears no rings. She rings the bell.

They wait for Olga, and waiting, Lucy thinks of stars. Stars up there, somewhere, wrapped in silence, wrapped in darkness. Flickering. Big ones, small ones, old and new, all moving, slowly, away from one another. Expanding. Then contracting. Like a heart.

Tea Party

The first thing Emma noticed when she opened the cottage door was the stillness. So quiet it was that she could hear one of Morgan's cows mooing in the back pasture over a mile away. Most days the wind blew, coming in from the Bristol Channel with such force that the trees along the channel cliffs grew sideways instead of straight, and nothing could be heard but the moan of the wind and the waves breaking against the rocks. Not that there was much worth listening to in St. Donat's. On the rare windless day you could hear the college clock chime the hour or the occasional car passing through on its way to Swansea. No one ever stopped in St. Donat's, but Emma couldn't blame them for that. There was nothing to stop for, not even a shop. Just the college, well hidden behind the castle walls, and outside, along the road, three houses, Morgan's farm, the tenant cottage, and the new college bungalow where the American lived.

The chickens scattered as Emma made her way across the yard to the small green door in the stone wall. She pulled the latch and, stopping, squeezed through the opening to stand by the road. She glanced across to see if the American might be watching, then looked both ways before crossing over. Though it was early yet for the cows to be brought home, Emma was taking no chances. It would not do for Owen to see her now. When she'd told him of the invitation the night before, at first he'd not believed her.

"She never! Making it up you are."

"I'm not!"

"The American is it then? The young one, looks like a stick?"

"Sweet looking she is."

"Sweet on me you mean. Every day I bring the cows by, she's at the window looking out. Fancies me she does."

"It might be you she fancies, but it's me she's asked to tea."

"Whatever for? She's got her fancy friends at College, doesn't she?"

"I wouldn't know I'm sure. But she was ever so friendly." Emma smiled. "She reminded me of Eleanor."

"Eleanor?"

"You know the one. The star on that American show, *Day without End.*"

"You and that frigging telly. I've a mind to take it back to rental. And you're not to go to tea as well."

Emma had looked over his shoulder at the green mold around the kitchen window and hadn't said a word.

He had no way of stopping her, but Emma knew what a noise he'd make if he caught her in the act. Not caring who heard either. So she looked both ways; there was nothing to be seen but puddles and cowpats. She crossed slowly, not wanting to appear too eager.

Rain was falling in a slow steady drizzle and Emma's mackintosh had long ago lost its waterproofing. Besides, it was so tight that she could no longer button up the front. She held the edges together as best she could, but even so could feel the wet seep through. Though she'd not weighed herself, Emma knew she'd gained at least a stone since they'd moved to St. Donat's the year before.

"If you'd do something besides watch the telly and eat sweets all day," Owen said.

"It's lonely I am, Owen. No one to talk to and not a car either."

"And what do you think I am then? Talking to Morgan's cows all day and another come evening."

"It would be lovely to have a car."

"Wouldn't it now? And I suppose you'd fancy a fridge and a gas cooker and a telephone too?"

"I wouldn't mind."

"My, such a lady I married and to think I never knew."

"It's important to broaden our horizons, Owen. Eleanor said so, just today."

Owen looked her up and down and laughed.

"You've broadened all right!" he said.

Emma sucked in her stomach as she walked up the American's drive. The girdle helped but not enough. She was trying to walk gracefully, but found it difficult when holding her breath; besides, the black stiletto heels made her ankles wobble. The American opened the door before Emma could knock.

"I'm so glad you could come," she said in a breathy sort of way.

"You're ever so nice to have me," Emma said, bobbing her head so that she could feel her little sausage curls dance.

As soon as Owen had left that morning, Emma had put up her hair, using every roller she had. It had been a morning of torture; not only were the rollers heavy, but they pinched and pulled each time she moved. Still, when at last she removed them, she was struck by the feeling of weightlessness. It made her feel like someone else.

"Come in," said the American. "Out of the rain." She smiled at Emma. "Isn't the weather depressing?"

"It is and all," said Emma, though the truth was she hadn't thought about the weather once all day.

They were standing in a large square hall with a shiny wood floor. There were four doorways leading off it, and stairs going up to a second floor as well.

Emma just had time to peek through the closest door. She saw a large white refrigerator next to a large white cooker and a round yellow-topped table, the same primrose yellow as the linoleum on the floor. With ruffled white curtains at the windows it looked like the kitchen of Emma's dreams.

"Here," said the American. "Let me take your coat."

She stood watching as Emma shrugged herself out of the old gray mackintosh. Emma felt her cheeks growing hot even though underneath the mackintosh she was wearing a respectable black jumper and a new plum-colored skirt bought in Cardiff the Saturday before. Owen had been rude about the skirt, telling her she hadn't the legs and was too old besides. The salesgirl had objected, saying she herself preferred "ample legs" like Emma's to the other legs one saw these days. Like bits of spaghetti, she said they were. As for being too old, Emma had seen plenty who were older walking about showing off their legs. The fact was she herself was only thirty-two.

She handed her mackintosh to the American.

"I like your skirt," the American said. "What a pretty color."

Emma smiled. "Plum it's called. And yours is ever so nice as well." It was a skirt like Emma's but plaid, a checkerboard of pale reds and greens. "Christmas colors," said Emma.

The American laughed. "I hadn't thought of that."

When she turned to hang Emma's coat in the closet, Emma glanced at her legs. Long and thin they were but shapely too, not at all like spaghetti. Once she'd hung the coat, the American led Emma directly into the sitting room, though Emma had hoped she first might show her about the house. When they had met on the road the day before, Emma, making conversation, asked how she liked the bungalow.

"It's a little too new," the American said.

"Is it now?" said Emma, baffled.

"You know what I mean about new houses? They haven't been lived in. They're just shells really. It takes years for a house to develop a soul."

"Fancy that," said Emma, who hadn't a clue what she meant. But she didn't mind not understanding, because all the time that they were talking Emma could feel horizons broadening.

Emma saw that the sitting room stretched the length of the house. Large and bright with red rugs on the floor and a picture window at either end. The back window looked over Morgan's pastures and the front looked across the road to Emma's cottage. Because of the wall surrounding the cottage, only the second floor with its two narrow windows set in the steeply pitched slate roof could be seen. With the moss on the roof and the gaps in the chimney where the bricks had fallen, the cottage looked as dreary out as in.

Mortified, Emma turned her back on the view and sat on a couch before the window. The American sat in an armchair facing her. Between them was a brightly polished table and to Emma's right, a slow-burning fire in the grate. The room seemed very warm to Emma and the fire not half hot enough to throw such heat.

"It's lovely warm in here," she said, smiling at the American.

"Goodness, do you think?" The American looked about, as if afraid someone might be listening, then turned to Emma. "I wouldn't say this to anyone from the college but you know, we were really surprised by the primitive central heating."

Emma blinked. The American leaned forward in her chair.

"I mean if it were an old house we'd understand, but to build a new house with a heating system that depends on a coal stove in the kitchen. . . ." She shrugged, then smiled. "It's not that I'm complaining. It's really a very nice house. I just haven't gotten used to being cold all the time."

Emma had no idea how central heating was supposed to work. In the cottage they had a coal-burning Aga for cooking and heating and one small electric fire that they moved from room to room. It never did much good unless you sat right in front and then it burned the legs.

"Do you cook on it too then?" she asked.

"On what?"

"The coal stove."

The American laughed. "Heavens no! There's a regular stove in the kitchen. Electric. I prefer gas, don't you?"

"I do and all," said Emma who had never cooked on anything but coal.

There was an uncomfortable silence. Emma knew that as the guest she should be making the conversation, but all she could think of was how badly she wanted to see the house. She crossed her legs, hoping to appear at ease, but uncrossed them quickly when she noticed how high the skirt rose on her thighs. Even with her legs straight she felt exposed, which made her wish she had her mackintosh to spread across her lap. The American, she noticed, had crossed her legs; if Emma wanted, she could have seen right to her panties. Instead she looked around the room. At the other end was a round dining table with six matching chairs and another small table that held the stereo. The white walls were hung with paintings and beneath them were white painted bookcases filled with books.

"My, it's a regular library you have," said Emma. "Did you bring the books with you from America then?"

"Oh no, we bought most of them here. They're much cheaper in this country, especially paperbacks." Leaning forward, she picked up a book from the coffee table and held it up for Emma to see. "This would have cost at least four dollars at home; here it's just two shillings, about fifty cents."

Emma looked at the book and felt the blush coming to her cheeks again. What a book to leave lying about for people to see. *Sons and Lovers* indeed! She never would have thought, from looking at her, that the American was the sort. Perhaps her husband then, but even so. The American was looking at Emma, obviously waiting for her to speak. Emma cleared her throat.

"Fancy that," she said. "I expect your husband must need a good many books for this teaching."

"Well, yes, he does need some. But I'm afraid most of them are mine." Replacing the book on the table, she smiled shyly. "I have a thing about books," she said.

Emma cleared her throat again. "Do you now?" she said.

The American nodded. "I need to read the way other people need to eat. Richard says it's avoidance."

Emma wished she hadn't mentioned eating because the word alone was enough to set her stomach grumbling.

"Everyone needs to eat," she said, "though my Owen, he never tires of telling me I eat more than my fair share." She patted her stomach. "I expect he's right and all."

"It's only because you're bored," she said, smiling at Emma so kindly that Emma couldn't help smiling in return.

Despite the book that lay on the table between them, she began to feel more comfortable. Lovely it was, thought Emma, to have a friend who understood. She settled back against the sofa and recrossed her legs.

"And how are you liking Wales then, Mrs. . . . ?"

"Robertson, but please, call me Lizard."

Emma's surprise must have shown because, laughing, Lizard ducked her head. When she looked up again, Emma saw that her cheeks were pink.

"My real name is Elizabeth, Liz for short. But when I was little everyone called me Lizard, and I'm afraid the name stuck."

"What an interesting name then," Emma said politely, knowing that never, even under torture, could she call her that.

"No it's not. It's ugly. But you know, I never really thought about it until I came over here. No one uses nicknames here. So usually I introduce myself as Elizabeth, unless I'm feeling relaxed and then I forget."

Emma couldn't help wondering what the American was like when she wasn't relaxed. She'd never seen anyone twitch so, always twiddling with her hair or nibbling at her fingernails. And the way she wriggled in the chair, crossing and uncrossing her legs, like a child who couldn't sit still.

Not that Emma minded, but she did find it surprising. She herself could sit motionless for hours at a time in front of the telly. The American, she supposed, was one of those high-strung types. On *Day without End* they were all a bit that way, crying and carrying on over trifles.

The American's face was thin and pale, the color of cream. A pretty face, but there was something, a certain softness in the wide eyes and the long fine hair that hung so straight down her back, that made her seem younger than she really was. She had no eyelashes that Emma could see; she was not even wearing lipstick. The only color in her face came from a dusting of light brown freckles across her nose.

She didn't look at all like Eleanor, who had sharp features and a regal air, but Emma realized that she'd been foolish to assume the American and Eleanor would be alike. She knew from watching the show that Americans could be as different from one another as the Welsh; only now she knew it in a new and special way.

Eleanor was fond of saying that real knowing came from what she called a "learning experience," and it came to Emma that this tea party with a real American was just that. She was learning through her own personal experience just how different Americans could be.

Emma was pleased she now knew exactly what Eleanor meant by a learning experience. And she was also pleased to discover that however exciting it might have been to have a friend as worldly as Eleanor, she was easier with this one.

All morning as she'd sat in front of the telly, head weighted with rollers, she had imagined how it would be, the two of them sipping tea from fragile china cups as they discussed the complications of Eleanor's life. Emma was sure the American would be impressed with how much she knew about American living. "Oh, not much at all, really," Emma had planned to say with becoming modesty.

But now that she was here, and as comfortable as she felt with her new friend, Emma could think of no way to casually introduce the subject. If only there were a telly in the sitting room, she could make a start by asking if it was color. She might even ask if they owned it instead of renting as Emma did. But there was no telly to be seen, and somehow it seemed forward to inquire.

Suddenly Emma realized that she'd said nothing for ages. It was one of her failings, going off inside her head that way, and it drove Owen bonkers. She looked at the American, who was staring at the fire, not seeming to mind the silence at all. Emma coughed politely, to attract attention.

"Your husband, is he liking to teach at college then?"

"Richard? Oh yes, I suppose." She began to fiddle with her hair. "He's busy; boarding schools are terrible that way. But then he likes being busy; he's very conscientious."

"And how about yourself, if you don't mind my asking. I should think it ever so interesting, being international. People to meet from all over the world."

"Actually, they're mostly British. We're the only Americans."

"You must be ever so popular then!"

"Why is that?" the American asked, looking puzzled.

"Being American and all. Such an interesting country I've always thought."

Emma waited for the American to ask her what she found interesting, but all she did was stare out the window over Emma's head. Emma's stomach began to rumble again, the way it always did when she was nervous. She coughed to cover the sound, wishing more than ever there was something to nibble. She had heard that Americans didn't have tea, not as a meal anyway. She hoped this wasn't true. The room was much too warm and Emma was beginning to sweat. Besides, the heat was causing her feet to swell so that the ache in her toes was worse than before. She was wondering if she might slip the heels off under the table when the American suddenly spoke.

"Do you know what I like best about living here?"

"What's that then?" Emma said, startled.

"To look out the window at your house."

Emma couldn't help herself; she laughed. "You never!"

The American nodded. "It's got such character, those narrow little windows and that steep roof. It's like something out of a fairy tale. I bet it's wonderful inside."

Was she hinting for a visit? The very thought made Emma blush for shame.

"Terrible it is. Terrible. Moss growing on the walls and the roof leaking day and night."

"But those things can be fixed, can't they?"

"It's Morgan's place, not ours, and not a shilling will he spend."

"Oh, what a shame! Surely if you talk to him?"

Emma snorted. "Easier talking to a stone. But never mind, it's moving we are, ever so soon, to one of the new council flats in Llantwit. Lovely they are with picture windows and all mod cons."

The American looked sadly at Emma. "Oh, I'm sorry," she said.

Just at that moment the kettle began to whistle from the kitchen.

"I'll be right back. You make yourself at home," the American said, smiling at Emma from the doorway.

Emma took several deep breaths to calm herself. She should not, she knew, have told the lie about the council flat, but she also knew that had the American asked her outright to visit the cottage, Emma, in all politeness, could not have refused. And it was not just the mold and the leaky roof that gave cause for shame, but all of it, from Owen's mucky boots at the door to their few sticks of furniture to the chipped mugs. They had had two teacups once, ever so sweet with pink roses, and delicate too, thin as tissue. But Owen had thrown one against the Aga in a rage and Emma had dropped the other on the floor. No, Emma decided, better to die from disease than the shame of such a visit.

Emma had to admit that despite her feelings of friendship for the American, she found her puzzling. Usually Emma took pride in her understanding of the people she met. Her Mum had always called Emma the "deep one," always said what a shame she'd not been able to stay in school past O levels. The trouble was Emma had never met anyone like this American, not even on the telly. What, for instance, did she mean by saying "I'm sorry" when Emma told her about the move to the council flat. Big and grand they were, modern as could be,

set right on the main road next to all the shops, and the cinema only
one street over.

The American returned with a large tray that she set down on the
table between them.

"I'm so glad you could come," she said as she began to dish up the
food.

And Emma realized then that the American had meant she was sorry
Emma would be moving away, just when they'd found each other too.

"What a lovely tea then!" Emma said with so much feeling in her
voice that the American looked up, startled.

It was a regular high tea with sandwiches and crisps, gherkins and
biscuits, even a sponge. The American smiled as she handed Emma
her plate.

"Why don't you start with this and then we can help ourselves to
seconds."

She had given Emma a bit of everything, all neatly arranged on a
gold-rimmed plate.

"Fancy your going to the trouble of cutting the crusts!" Emma said
as she picked up a dainty triangle of bread.

"It wasn't any trouble. I hope you like watercress."

Emma swallowed first, careful to chew with her mouth closed.

"My personal preference," she said, "though it's seldom I see it. My
Owen now, he likes his fishpaste so that's what we get. Fishpaste or
Marmite."

"Richard likes Marmite too. Isn't it awful?"

"It is and all. Nasty brown stuff, more like medicine than food, I'd
say."

They smiled at each other. As Emma helped herself to another sandwich, she noticed the American was only toying with her food, pushing
it about on her plate with her finger.

"Don't mind me," she said when she saw Emma looking. "I'm
never hungry at teatime."

"It's not a meal you have in American then," Emma said, pleased to
be able to show off her knowledge.

"No. I was amazed to find people over here eating four meals a day."

"It's the boredom, I expect," said Emma.

"What?"

"What you said before, about eating being a way to pass the time and all."

"Oh. But everybody can't be bored, can they?"

"There's truth in that, I suppose," Emma said, taking another sandwich. Without the crusts, two bites, and it was gone. "You must have ever so much to keep you busy, with a car to take you places and interesting friends at college."

She tried to chew more slowly, but this was difficult as she was hungry.

"They're very nice, most of them. But they're busy; all the ones my age have little children."

"Children can be a terrible nuisance," Emma said, eyeing the teapot. Her throat was parched from conversation.

"That's what Richard says. He says we should wait. But. . . ."

She couldn't seem to find the words. Instead she shrugged her shoulders and stared into the fire.

"And right he is," Emma said kindly, but firmly. "Oldest of nine I was and changing nappies before I walked. 'Never again,' I said to Owen, and he agreed. Hard it is to get ahead in this world with babies holding you down."

"I suppose so, but . . ." she looked at Emma, shyly, and laughed, "I never knew days could be so long."

"*Day without End,*" Emma said, pleased to have found an opening.

She popped a crisp into her mouth, something she hadn't dared do before because of the noise they made when chewed, and held it on her tongue to soften.

"I knew you'd understand," the American said. "That's it exactly. Days without end. Richard doesn't understand at all. He just gets cross."

"My Owen's the same, goes on and on he does. I suppose," she said casually, "you watch a good deal then?"

"Watch what?"

"Why the telly. *Day without End* and all."

The American looked puzzled. "I can't say that I do," she said. "I've never liked television much."

"Is that a fact?"

The American nodded.

"I thought it would be better over here, but it's mostly American stuff and the worst of it at that. Like *Day without End.* Isn't that one of those awful soaps?"

Emma cleared her throat. "I expect it is and all."

"The people at College watch the news and get the impression that the States is nothing but muggings and killings and riots in the streets."

"Oh but surely they know better than that!"

The American smiled at Emma. "You'd think so, wouldn't you?"

"I would. Ever so lovely it is, I'm sure."

"You don't have to go that far," said the American, laughing, and Emma laughed too, so as not to seem rude.

"Are you ready for tea?"

"Yes, please," said Emma.

The American poured the tea into two white cups, as fragile as the ones Emma had imagined. It was a shame they would not be discussing *Day without End,* but glad she was she'd not made a fool of herself by admitting she watched it.

The American held her teacup with the little finger extended and Emma did the same.

"What do you do, to keep busy?" the American said.

Emma took several swallows of her tea before answering. "Oh, I putter about. Bursar from the college, he came by last week to offer me work, but Owen said no to that, thank you but no; he wants me home."

"That's sweet," the American said.

Emma stared at her to see if she joking. "I wouldn't know about that," she said. "He likes his tea on time, he does."

"Richard eats most of his meals up at school."

"Lucky you are. Plenty of time to get off on your own."

"That's what Richard says."

"What's that then?"

"That I'm fortunate to have so much time on my hands and I should take advantage of it."

"And right he is. Why, if I had a car, there'd be no stopping me. All I'd need is a friend for company." Emma, her cheeks flushed with warmth and pleasure, smiled at her friend while she waited for the invitation she knew was coming.

Perhaps, she thought, they could go for a spin this very afternoon.

Drive right past Owen as he was bringing home the cows. Lovely little red Morris Minor the American had and Emma could just imagine the look on Owen's face when he saw who was inside it. Emma waited, but the American, instead of asking, stared at Emma without smiling. The look made Emma uncomfortable. Had she been too forward, made her wishes too plain? The American suddenly leaned toward Emma.

"What would you do if you had a car?" she asked, her voice quiet and curious.

"Why, what wouldn't I do! I'd get out, I would, away from all that." Emma waved her hand in the direction of her cottage. "I'd go to Cardiff one day, Swansea the next. With some experience, I might drive to London on the motorway."

"And then what?"

Emma blinked. It occurred to her to wonder if the American was quite right in the head. Ashamed of such an unkind thought, instead of answering she took a bite of sponge.

"This sponge is ever so nice," she said, forgetting to swallow first. The yellow crumbs sprayed onto her lap. "Oh dear," she said, but the American didn't notice at all. Her eyes were still on Emma's face.

"No, really, I'm curious. What would you do when you'd finished driving around?"

"Why, I suppose I'd come home again, wouldn't I?" Emma said with a snap in her voice.

The American didn't mind; in fact from the way she was nodding her head up and down, she seemed pleased with Emma's answer.

"That's right. That's the problem. No matter how far I go, I can't escape. It doesn't matter where I am, I'm always trapped. The loneliness, it's inside, you see."

Her voice had gone quite thick and Emma realized with dismay that at any moment she might start to cry. She would not, Emma knew, cry in ladylike fashion like Eleanor, and Emma felt herself being torn in two; half of her wanted to stay with this strange new friend and give what comfort she could, the other half wanted to bolt for home. The gold clock on the mantel struck four as Emma sat there, undecided.

The American looked up at the clock. "Heavens, is it four o'clock already?" Clearing her throat, she turned to Emma. "Your husband will be coming with the cows."

"He will and all and I best be going. Likes his tea on time he does."

Rising, the American went to stand by the window. Emma stood behind her, shifting her weight from one foot to the other in an attempt to lessen the pain in her toes.

"Thanks ever so," she said to the American's back. "And if it's company you'd be wanting when you're off in your car, I'd be happy to. . . ."

"Look," said the American. "Here he comes!"

Emma, taking care to stand out of sight, watched as the cows passed down the lane. They moved slowly, milling and mooing, their heads lowered, tails flicking. Behind them walked Owen, a switch in his hand, his head bent forward against the rain. One cow stopped short and Owen whacked it hard on the rump, cursing in Welsh. Emma was glad for the Welsh, but the noise of him was bad enough.

"Walks just like one of the cows he does," she said, embarrassed by the mud caking his Wellingtons, the slouch of his shoulders, his tangled hair. "Could do with a haircut as well," she said.

"Oh no!" said the American, turning to Emma. "I love the way he looks."

"Do you now?" Emma said, standing straight as she could and looking the American in the eye. Because the American was several inches taller, Emma had to look up, but even so the American became agitated. She looked away from Emma, her cheeks red.

"Oh, I don't mean it like that! Not that he isn't good-looking; he is, very. But what I like is how natural he seems, so much a part of his surroundings. Maybe earthiness is the best word to describe him."

Earthiness indeed, thought Emma as she moved toward the hall closet to fetch her mackintosh. Just wait till Owen heard that what the American fancied was the mud on his trousers. Insulting as it was to both of them, Emma couldn't wait to tell him, just to see the look on his face. The American followed her into the hall.

"Do you know what I mean?" she said as Emma pulled on her coat. "It's the same way I feel about your house, a sense of belonging in a way that ours doesn't, and we don't either."

Emma, coat on at last, turned to face her.

"Thanks ever so. It was a lovely tea."

The American looked worried. "I haven't said anything wrong, have I?"

And from the tone of her voice, Emma knew that however insulting she had been, it had not been intentional. As she opened the front door, Emma smiled. "Not to worry," she said.

"Oh, I am glad!" the American said. "I knew you'd understand."

There was no answer to that so Emma bobbed her head once before closing the door. She walked quickly down the drive and across the road, knowing that if she hurried she could catch the last five minutes of *Day without End*.

Kiss the Father

"Kiss your father," said the mother. She held the father in her hands, and the child kissed the cold glass face. "Careful," said the mother. The child felt the glass grow warm, hot where she touched it. The mother put the father back, high up on the bureau.

"This little piggy," said the mother, setting the child in her lap. She tweaked her toes. The child laughed. The mother laughed too. "This is the way the ladies ride," said the mother. The room bounced up and down.

"What's this!" said the grandmother. The child smelled flowers. She waved her hands. "Poor babes in the woods," sang the grandmother, "poor babes in the woods." Her voice was a cloud.

"Rockaby baby, on the tree tops," they sang. The child rocked in the grandmother's arms. The room rocked too. Gently. "And down will come baby. . . ." Down, down floated the child, into the dark.

In the morning there was light. There were hands, lifting, and a face. The child saw ears, eyes, nose, mouth. She knew them and they knew her. "Mouth!" said the child. The mouth smiled. The child poked a finger in the mouth. Teeth bit, gently. The child laughed. "Teeth!" she said, and arms hugged her. "Listen to you!" said the mouth, laughing. The child listened. She heard soft breathing, in and out. "Mommy," she said. "Mommy."

Everywhere there was light. The child held the spoon. The spoon went up and down, the cereal sliding into her mouth, sweet and warm, down, down. "All gone," sang the child. The rabbit smiled in the bowl. The child licked his warm smooth face.

The child sat on the mother's bed. The mother slipped a piece of paper on her hand and rubbed her leg. "Hisssss," went the paper, round and round. "All done," said the mother. The child held the leg. She rubbed her cheek against it, up and down. "Mine!" she said. The mother laughed.

Light danced on the water. The sand was warm. "Mommy," said the child. "Hmmm," said the mother. Her eyes were closed. The child sat on warm sand next to the mother. She watched the water dance. She saw the trees clapping their hands.

Hands lifted her from bed and laid her down. Up and down. There was dark and there was light. In the warm dark Uncle held her. "The moon!" said Uncle. He held her up. His hands held her. He walked her on his feet. Up and down went their feet together, higher and higher. She laughed and laughed. "Time for bed," said the mother. "Kiss your father good night." The child cried. She kissed the father. His face was wet. The mother wiped the father's face and put him back, high up on the bureau.

The dark was light. Light fell through the door into the room. The child reached through the bars to catch the light. She felt it slipping through her fingers. "Mommy," she sang, "Mommy." The mother broke the soft light into ribbons. "Shh," said the mother. "Shh," said the water. "Shhhh," said the trees. Soft voices rose and fell. The piano played far far away.

GIDDIUP, GIDDIUP, GIDDIUP said the train. The train rocked back and forth. The mother and the child rocked in the bed. Rocked and rocked. The child touched the mother's leg. The leg was smooth and warm. The bed was warm. It smelled like soap. It smelled like milk. The light was green.

The apartment was hot. The child sat at the window. She looked down and down. Back and forth went the cars on the street, back and forth. The child sat way up high. Hot air blew up between her legs. She poked her fingers through the hard warm squares. She felt the hot.

"Kiss your father good night," the mother said. She lifted the child down. The father sat on the table. The fire crackled. The light made shadow on Gran-Gran's face. She smelled like dust. "No," said the child.

"Oh, this war," said Gran-Gran.

"How could she know," said the mother. "She's hardly two."

The mother kissed the father. "Like this," she said. The child kissed the cold glass. "Good girl," said the mother. She danced the child across room. "Pack up your troubles in an old kit bag," she sang. Her hair danced, tickling. The child laughed. "That's better," said Gran-Gran.

Out the door there was a hall with plants in pots, and green vines growing up the walls, and a red button. "Push it," said the mother. The elevator was small. The women wore fur coats, and smelled like powder. Their hands were wrinkled. The elevator man had a gold chain, and a lollipop in his pocket. "Who's been a good girl?" said the elevator man. "Me! Me!" sang the child. The fur coats laughed. The lollipop was orange. "That's why your daddy's coming home," said the elevator man. The child licked and licked until the lollipop was all gone.

"Kiss your father," said the mother. The child sat at the window. She saw the snow slip from the sky. Down and down.

Hands caught her, tossed her in the air. She fell, crying, and up she went again. Hands caught her.

"Does she always cry?"

"She doesn't know you yet."

The hands carried her, kicking, to the table. The father sat on the table. "Show me the eyes." The child pointed. She pointed at the eyes and the nose and the mouth. "Show me the uniform."

"No," said the child.

"She doesn't know the word," said the mother.

The hands turned her around. "Look at me," said the man. The child looked. "That's me in the picture," said the man. "I'm your father." The child sucked her thumb. The father sat on the table, and the man said, "Say daddy."

"Daddy," said the child around the thumb.

"She's learning," said the man. His mouth smiled, but not his eyes. He sat the child on the sofa. Her legs stuck out. She looked at her sandals. She wiggled her toes but couldn't see them. The man danced the mother up and down the room. "Rosein the bud, the Juneair's warmandtender," he sang. The mother laughed. Gran-Gran sat on the sofa and blew her nose.

"Me!" said the child. She pushed his legs. He was a mountain. He did not move. "Me!" she cried.

The man bent down. His hot breath was on her cheek. He smelled of smoke. "You have to learn to share!" he said.

"Rise and shine," said the father. The pipes gurgled. The room was hot. "Mommy," said the child. The shades rattled up. "Mommy." Out the window she saw falling snow. The light was gray. A dog barked once. It was the man; his laugh was sharp.

"She's sick," he said. "She has the measles. We don't want you to get sick too."

The door was closed. "Mommy!" she cried. She rattled the knob. She kicked her sandals against the wood. Her toes hurt. The child cried.

The father filled the door. "Shame on you!" he said. She hit his legs with her hands. Her hands hurt. Through the legs she saw the mother in the bed. "She doesn't understand," said the mother.

"She'll understand this," the father said. He raised his hand.

"Don't," said the mother.

The door closed. The child sucked her thumb and cried.

The room was dark. There was no light at all. "Mommy!" called the child. "Mommy." She sang the word. The door opened. The father stood in the light. "You go to sleep!" he said. The shadow climbed the wall. The child saw ears and a pointed nose. She saw fur. The shadow opened his mouth. The teeth were sharp. "Be good," said the father, "and we'll bring you a present from New York." He raised his hand. It was a claw. It touched her face. The door closed. It was dark.

There were two heads in the mother's bed. Then there were none. The sheets were cold. The child climbed up and up. She held the mother's pillow. She smelled the mother. She smelled smoke.

"So that's where you are!" Minnie's fingers pinched. "Sneaking into other people's rooms." Her clothes crackled. There were whiskers on her chin. She sniffed. "It's not as if they'd gone forever."

Her knees were sharp. Minnie turned the page. "'Why, what big teeth you have, Grandma!' said Little Red Riding Hood. 'THE BETTER TO EAT YOU WITH!' cried the wolf, and he jumped out of bed, and he ate Little Red Riding Hood ALL UP."

The child opened her mouth and cried. She cried and cried. Minnie slapped the book shut. "I know someone who's had too much excitement!" She pinched the child's nose. The cold green taste slid down into her stomach. The cold green taste went up her nose. She cried.

"Someone I know is spoiled," said Minnie. Her breath gurgled. She tapped the spoon against the bowl. "EATITUP! EATITUP!" she said. She smacked her lips. The child swallowed. The cereal stayed in her mouth. "Whatever next," said Minnie.

"Fresh air," said Minnie. Her fingers buttoned, snapped, tugged, pinched, pulled. They went down and down. "How about a lollipop?" said the elevator man.

Minnie sniffed. "No treats," she said. "This one didn't eat her breakfast."

Snow blew this way and that. Smoke puffed from Minnie's mouth. The child stuck out her tongue to catch the snow. The snow pricked; then it was gone. "Where are your manners!" Minnie said. She pulled the child across the street.

"Why, Minnie McKay," said the fat man. His stomach went up and down when he laughed. "You come for a skate around my rink?"

Minnie sniffed. "I wouldn't say no."

"Who's this then?" said the fat man. The hand patted the child's head.

"The war makes orphans of us all," said Minnie. She sniffed.

"Poor little tyke."

"I do my best," said Minnie.

The fat man held Minnie's arm. They slid away. The child stood on glass. She sucked her mitten. She looked down at the glass. She saw a face. She saw eyes, nose, mouth. She moved closer. The face moved closer too. "Kiss," she said. The mouth opened; the teeth were white. She felt glass slide beneath her boots. She fell down. Her head bumped. Hard.

The child lay on her back. There was snow in her eyes. "Maybe she's hurt," the fat man said. He picked her up. "She should be crying."

Minnie sniffed. Her hands spun the child, dusting. "Hurt!" she said. She sniffed again.

"This is your house," said Gran-Gran. The child lay on the rug. Gran-Gran put a sheet over the table. The sheet was white. The child sucked her thumb. The white was all around.

"Your trick, Helen," said Gran-Gran.

Cards slapped the table. The table shivered.

"Isn't she good."

"So quiet."

"Minnie's a treasure."

"When?"

"Next week."

"Such a shame. Two weeks of leave, and one spent in bed with the measles."

"We do what we can."

"Does she miss her mother, do you think?"

"Heavens, no! She's much too young!"

EATITUP, EATITUP, EATITUP said the train. The child sat on the green seat. The seat scratched her legs. "Mareseatoats and lambseatoats and little lambseativy," sang the mother. She held out her arms. "We're going to see Daddy soon," she sang. The child looked out the window. EATITUP, EATITUP sang the train. The sky was gray. She saw a car. The car was gone. A tree. A cat. A mother. A child. EATITUP.

Fathers walked up and down the train. They wore uniforms and their teeth were sharp.

"Don't you want to sit on my lap?" the mother said.

The child pressed her forehead to the glass. The glass was cold. She smelled the father. The mother smelled like the father too. So did the train. The glass shivered her head. The train ate up a house. Her ears hurt. She did not cry.

"If only it wasn't so small," said the mother.
"At least we're together," said the father.
The child lay in a crib. Her ears hurt. She did not cry. She climbed up and up, and down. She climbed into the big bed. The father woke up. "Oh, no you don't," he said. His hands lifted her up. She closed her eyes. She felt the crib around her.
"She's asleep."
The light was gray. There were no windows. The child watched the big bed rise and fall. She heard the wolf groan. The mother disappeared. The child closed her eyes. She rubbed her arm against her face. She rubbed and rubbed. The arm grew warm. She smelled the warm skin. She knew the smell. It was her smell. She smelled and smelled. Her ears roared. She did not cry.

The doctor wore white. There was glass on his eyes. He said, "Hold her tight." The mother held the child tight. Her ears roared. They went hot and wet. They slept.
"She didn't even cry," said the mother.
"There's my soldier," said the father.
The child sat on his lap. She did not move. "You deserve a treat," said the father. He opened the book.
"'WHO'S BEEN SLEEPING IN *MY* BED!'" roared the father in a Daddy Bear voice.
The child shook. She could not stop shaking. Her teeth went click-click. Her arms were cold. Her head was hot. Her ears roared. The mother put her hand on the child's forehead. "It's that fever again."

The child slept. She woke and smelled her arm. She slept. The doctor came. Her ears roared and grew hot and wet. The father sat by the crib. "This is terrible," he said. The bars made ribbons down his face. "When you're better," he said, "I'll take you to my ship." The father went away. The child smelled her arm. She slept and slept.

The father carried her down the hill. "She doesn't weigh a thing," he said. On his shoulder her head went back and forth. "She's still weak," said the mother. They walked and walked. The sun was warm. A tree clapped its hands. She smelled the water. "Sand," said the child.

"Imagine!" said the mother. "She's remembering Florida. She was only a baby."

"She's lucky," said the father. "She won't remember any of this."

The ship was gray. Fathers marched up and down. They stood still. They raised their hands. The child closed her eyes.

"Here's the story," said the father. "While we have lunch with the captain, you get to sleep in my bed."

"No," said the child.

"Let me," said the mother.

"I'll handle this."

The mother disappeared. The father marched down the stairs. Bang bang bang went his shoes. He held the child tight. They went down and down.

The room was small. The walls were gray. The bed was hard. "You're a lucky girl," said the father. "Go right to sleep." The door closed.

The child did not close her eyes. She did not move. She heard fathers shouting. She heard feet running up and down.

On the wall she saw the mother. The mother was smiling. The child touched her. The mother was cold. "Mommy," said the child. The mother smiled. Her teeth were white. She did not say a word.

Question of Light

There is the question of light. Mary Beth lies on her bed and watches the headlights of passing cars sweep across the ceiling. They travel slowly to the top of the door. When the cars turn the corner, the lights disappear. She lies in the darkness, waiting.

The windows are closed and the room is hot. She wonders if it is still snowing. The door is closed too. Through the wall she hears the high whine of her daughter's hair dryer, from the floor below the savage sounds of her son's rock group rehearsing. The vibrations travel up through the floor to shiver the flowers on the bedside table. The windows rattle.

She lies in bed, waiting for the song to end, waiting for silence to come again.

Dr. Green had looked at her in silence this afternoon. Behind him, she saw snow falling on the city streets. He cleared his throat. "Go home," he said. He looked at her; he looked at Richard. "Enjoy yourselves." He smiled, and Mary Beth saw his eyes were bright with tears.

Outside the hospital, on the same corner where they had stood so many times before, Richard turned to Mary Beth. "Will you be okay?" he said. He wore a black suit and his face was pale. He carried his briefcase in his hand. Mary Beth watched the stoplight shift from red to green, colors muted by the drifting snow. When she nodded, he nodded too. "I'll be home by seven," he said.

It's almost six. Mary Beth waits for her stomach to tell her she is hungry. Instead it cramps, a twist of pain. She remembers when the pain was bad, remembers the measure of those days. She eases onto her side to face the door. Lights sweep across it. Out on the street the sound of tires are muffled by the snow. A snowplow rumbles by. She remembers, as a child, the sound of chains, the grate of metal sparking blue. She remembers dreams of snowplows that scooped her screaming into gaping mouths. She hears the snow tires whispering, feels the throbbing of Ben's electric bass beating inside her like a heart.

The pain subsides: it's only hunger after all.

The phone rings by the bed. Mary Beth lets it ring six times, knowing as she picks it up who it will be. She knows it will be Sarah, but she does not know what to say.

"Bethie?" Sarah's voice is soft and husky. "How are you?" It is a huskiness that comes from smoking. They are the same age, thirty-eight, and Sarah has been smoking for twenty years.

"You smoke too much, you know," says Mary Beth. She is careful to keep her voice light. Slowly she straightens her legs, but the end of the bed is cold. She curls into a ball. One hand holds the phone, the other traces the thin ridged scar across her chest.

Sarah laughs, but Mary Beth hears her irritation. She does not like to be nagged about her smoking. "Well?" she says. She pauses. Mary Beth says nothing. She strokes the scars; she strokes them the way she stroked her blanket as a child. "Did you see him?" says Sarah.

"I saw him," says Mary Beth.

"Well?"

The room is dark. Mary Beth closes her eyes to make it darker.

"Sarah," she says. "Do you know we've been friends for twenty years?"

"For God's sake, Mary Beth! The tests! The doctor! What did he say?"

Mary Beth imagines Sarah hunched over the phone. She imagines her smoking, imagines that because it's six and she's been worrying, she's probably drinking too.

"How much sherry have you had?" Mary Beth smiles, anticipating her anger.

"Damn it, will you answer me? I've waited all day!" Her voice goes high.

"I'm sorry," says Mary Beth. She is. It's unforgivable that she should cause her best friend pain. "Don't, Sarah, please. It's all right. It's just. . . ." She stops, surprised. She touches her cheek. Her face is wet. She can't remember when she last cried. "It's just. . . ." But she can't say it. "Sarah," she says, "it's been seven years, Sarah. Do you think seven is a magic number?"

"Mary Beth, is Richard home?" Sarah sounds alarmed. Mary Beth cradles the phone against her ear.

"Richard always comes home at seven," says Mary Beth. "You know that."

"The children?" says Sarah.

Mary Beth hears her son's rock band breaking up. She hears doors slamming, sees headlights slide across the ceiling. "Sarah," she says, "do you remember tire chains, that awful noise?"

"Jesus," says Sarah. "You stay put. I'm coming over."

"Where would I go?" says Mary Beth, but Sarah's hung up. The line is dead.

The door opens. A wedge of light cuts through the room. Her son slouches, a silhouette against the light. He is taller than Richard now; Mary Beth is not sure how it happened. "We didn't bother you, Ma," he says, a statement, not a question. He is a diplomat, skilled in evasion. His voice is hoarse from singing. He leans against the door. "I'm taking off," he says. "You want anything before I go?"

Because the light is behind him, Mary Beth can't see his face. But she remembers how clear his eyes were as a baby.

"Honey," she says. "Stay and talk."

"Ma!" He steps backward into the hall. "The guys are waiting."

Mary Beth sighs. "Drive carefully," she says, but he's already gone, leaving behind a smell of unwashed socks.

The door is open. She hears Melissa talking on the phone. "You're kidding!" she shrieks. Her laughter is high-pitched, hysterical. Mary Beth can't imagine what she finds so funny: as a child Melissa never laughed at all.

The children had been Richard's idea. "To keep you company," he said. It was before they'd moved to Boston, when they'd lived outside St. Louis. Richard traveled, returning home on weekends. All week Mary Beth waited. The earth was flat and all around was sky. She played the piano and watched clouds moving. She copied recipes, but never cooked because the house had been in Richard's family for three generations, and family servants ran the house. On Friday she washed her hair and was dressed by noon in case he came home early. Sitting on the porch, she waited, a book open on her lap.

"My little Scarlett," he said. He kissed her gently. He smelled of travel. She smelled of lilacs. She was small-boned with dark hair and pearly skin. His hands met around her waist. Her father had called her Angel Face, my little princess. Richard called her Precious.

"My little mother," he called her when Ben was born.

She didn't feel like a mother, but all the same when Ben was five weeks old, he smiled at her, a tenuous smile that settled in her stomach, filling a hole she had not known existed. Maybe, she'd thought, everything would be all right. He cried infrequently, but when he did all she had to do was sing, and he'd fall silent, listening.

Melissa never listened. Melissa cried, her screams piercing, sharp as thorns. "Colic," the doctor said. When Mary Beth tried to hold her, she went stiff, legs rigid, small fists beating air. When she cried, Mary Beth cried too. She cried, "I wasn't meant to be a mother." The next day Richard hired a nurse.

Melissa hangs up. Mary Beth hears her singing in her room, hears her opening and closing bureau drawers. Mary Beth wonders what she's looking for. She wonders who she is. Her children. They are bright shadows that flit along the wall. When she reaches out to touch them, they are gone.

She remembers, after the second operation, Melissa standing by her bed, remembers how she stared, her eyes round as pennies, her thick hair shining. "Tell your mother you love her," said Richard, but Melissa had pointed at the pillow. "She's falling apart," she said, accusing, and lifting her head, Mary Beth saw her own hair lying in dark drifts across the pillow.

"Shame on you," said Richard.

"Never mind," said Mary Beth. She looked at him. "She's right."

Melissa calls out as she leaps past the open door. "Hi Mom," she says. "How you feeling?" She doesn't wait for an answer, but by now Mary Beth doesn't expect her to. She hears her bounding down the stairs, returning with laundry in her arms. "See you, Mom," she says. What Mary Beth sees is the curve of breasts beneath her turtleneck, and she tries to think. Is she thirteen now, or fourteen? How terrible that she doesn't know.

"Where are you going, darling?" says Mary Beth. "Come give me a kiss."

Melissa blows a quick kiss from the door. Like Richard, she has always shied from physical affection; even as a child she'd never do more than kiss the air near Mary Beth's cheek. She stands in the doorway, balanced on one leg like a stork. Mary Beth would like to say something that will bring her closer, but does not know what that something is.

She's relieved to hear the sound of Sarah's car turn in the driveway, until she remembers why Sarah has come.

She's not been able to think about the visit this afternoon with Dr. Green; there is no place to store the information.

It is easier, far easier, to think instead of the visit two months ago that followed a CAT-scan of her brain.

"Precautionary measures," Dr. Green had said when she'd complained of headaches, of flashing lights before her eyes.

Afterward they sat, as they always sat, in his office, his desk between them. "I'm afraid there seems to be a tumor in there." He said it softly, glaring at the wall above her head. For the first time in seven years there was no mention of an operation.

Inoperable. It had never happened to Mary Beth before. She imagined the tumor nestled in her brain like a maggot in cheese. "We'll keep a close eye," he said. "Every two weeks I want you in for tests."

Mary Beth hears Sarah's car door closing. Perhaps, she thinks, I'm in a state of shock. For seven years she has been riveted to the present, to the precise events that make a single day.

She's heard that sometimes, in the moment of dying, the past rises to surface like a leaf on water. But four years ago when she came close to death, it had been nothing like that. There had been only the sensation of being sucked down a dark tunnel toward a greater darkness, and it seemed that only Sarah's arms had held her back.

"Here's your best friend," Melissa says. Her voice is scornful, but it's hard to tell if the scorn is for Mary Beth, or for Sarah who is her friend.

Sarah doesn't notice. She stands in the doorway, her hand resting on Melissa's shoulder. "Why is your mother lying in the dark?"

Melissa shrugs. "Don't ask me." She smiles, wary, at Sarah, whom she likes even though she doesn't want to. "I gotta be going," she says. "See you."

"Kids!" Sarah laughs as she comes into the room. "It blows my mind to see them turning into real people."

Sarah has five, all boys with sturdy legs and swinging hair. Sometimes she says, joking, that Mary Beth is the daughter she never had. She sits on the edge of the bed and puts her arm around Mary Beth.

"So how's it going?" she says, her voice both tough and sweet. It's all Mary Beth can do not to cry. She shrugs. Her shoulder feels small under Sarah's large hand. In fact it is. Sarah is large all over without being fat.

Richard has always referred to them as Mutt and Jeff. "Fuck off," says Sarah, laughing, but Mary Beth knows she's not amused. She's never liked Richard. "A tight ass," she called him the first time they met, and though Sarah has probably forgotten, Mary Beth has not.

"Let's have some light," says Sarah. She flicks on the small lamp beside the bed. Mary Beth screws up her eyes, and Sarah reaches out to touch her cheek. "You've been crying," she says. "Bad news, huh?"

It's the gentle touch that undoes Mary Beth. Tears roll down her face. All she can do is shake her head.

"Oh, honey," says Sarah. She puts both arms around her, and holds her close. Her sweater smells of cigarettes. "Shit!" she says. "Goddamn shit!"

She rocks Mary Beth back and forth. Both of them are crying. Crying, Mary Beth tries to imagine how it would have been had their roles been reversed, if Sarah had been dying, and it had been her role to comfort. She can imagine neither.

She has often longed to say "You are the best thing that ever happened to me," but she is too shy. Instead she gives her presents, small bright things, bracelets, rings, enameled boxes. Mary Beth loves to watch her opening presents, the way she flings off the paper, squealing at whatever is revealed. Her pleasure is childlike, infectious. Mary Beth loves to give her presents. She has never understood why Sarah wants to be her friend.

Seven years ago, when the first lump was discovered, it was Richard who took her to the hospital, Sarah who waited. Mary Beth was frightened, but not surprised. It was that year she had felt herself unraveling. Both children were in school, and each day she wandered through the house, from room to room, touching things, to make sure that she, not they, existed.

"Aren't you the lucky one," the nurse said when it was over. "Your friend's been waiting here all day." She flipped Mary Beth as if she were a doll, straightening the sheet beneath her.

"My roommate," said Mary Beth. Her voice was thick. She felt the pain beneath the anesthetic. "From college."

"Lucky you," the nurse said. She raised the white sides of the narrow bed. "A short visit now. Then beddy bye."

Sarah sat by the bed and held Mary Beth's hand through the bars. The nurse had strapped her down so she wouldn't jar the stitches as she slept. Beyond the straps were bars. Sarah's hand was warm. The room was small with one thin window. The walls were white, the pure white of falling snow.

Richard cast a shadow on the wall. He stood above her, his arm stiff, holding flowers. It hurt her eyes to look. His face was white, the roses red, the color of blood. She smiled anyway.

"You've been so brave," he said in his stiff voice with something like surprise.

She was brave. So brave. Before the operation, and after. Through all the operations that followed.

For seven years she has been almost happy.

"Oh, Sarah," she cries, pressing her face against the sweater.

"Shh," says Sarah, rocking her like a baby, the way Mary Beth once rocked Ben, singing to his listening eyes. But Sarah doesn't sing. She says, "This is the pits!"

Mary Beth lets herself be rocked. She thinks of pits, a peach pit, pock-marked, buried in her brain.

Two months before, when it had been discovered, Dr. Green had frowned at her. "We'll just have to hope for the best," he said.

"It's all right," said Mary Beth, because she knew he was upset.

But it hadn't been all right at all. For seven years they'd been a team. She had only to feel the slightest pain, and he would find the source and pluck the poison from her body. His touch meant more to her than Richard's.

"It's all right," she said. "It's not the dying . . . but what if I go crazy?"

"You won't," he said, so quickly that she knew she could.

Standing, he put his arm around her. "There's my little warrior," he said.

"What if I do?" she said.

He squeezed her shoulder, opened the door. "Trust me," he said.

She wanted to. Dr. Green has a kind, shy smile, and hair like silver wire. He's old enough to be her father, but her heart beats faster when she sees him.

She can't imagine life without him. She can't imagine life at all.

Sarah stops rocking. "Bethie," she says, "do the children know?"

Mary Beth, leaning against her, remembers seven years ago when she first told Ben. "Honey," she said, "there's something wrong." He was sitting at the piano, small hands poised above the keys. "I have to have an operation." His eyes were cloudy, but when she told him the veil lifted, and for an instant she glimpsed the terror underneath. Then the cloudiness returned. "I gotta practice, Mom," he said.

"No," says Mary Beth. "Not yet."

Sarah leans away from Mary Beth, and plucking a Kleenex from the box beside the bed, blows her nose. "Christ," she says. She lights a cigarette. The smoke drifts toward the lamp. The light glows like sunset through the ruffled shade. Mary Beth watches.

"Is it still snowing?"

"Nope," says Sarah. "It's beautiful. I never saw so many stars."

Mary Beth hears a car pull in the driveway. She knows it's Richard. She hears the careful closing of the door, the snow squeaking as he walks toward the house. She knows that time is running out.

"Sarah," she whispers. "You're the best thing that ever happened to me." There is sudden lightness in her, the relief of having said it at last.

"Dummy." Sarah is embarrassed. She gives Mary Beth a hug, a careful hug, as if afraid of breaking her. "It's been real," she says.

They sit, listening to Richard walking through the house downstairs.

"Does he know?" says Sarah, whispering too.

Mary Beth nods.

They hear him coming up the stairs. There is the sound of something tinkling, glass or ice. He appears in the doorway, his cheeks pinched with cold, his coat still on. He is carrying a small tray that holds three glasses and a bottle of champagne.

Sarah stares as Richard places the tray on the bedside table and bends to loosen the cork.

"Maybe you'd like to tell me what we're celebrating?" says Sarah, her voice pungent with dislike.

Richard looks surprised. "She didn't tell you?" He aims the bottle at the ceiling. The cork explodes. Hitting the ceiling, it falls on Mary Beth's bed. He looks at Mary Beth, who takes the cork and holds it to her mouth. "My lips are sealed," she says. She feels the air escaping as she speaks.

Richard shakes his head. He looks at Sarah. "Maybe she wanted to surprise you."

Sarah stands up. She frowns at Richard. "You're spilling that." She takes the bottle from him. Champagne foams from the top. Richard cups his hands around the glasses as Sarah pours. Mary Beth watches the bubbles rising. "Careful," says Sarah. "It's full." She hands a glass to Mary Beth. Their fingers touch, then slide apart. The glass is cold.

Richard smiles at Sarah. "To life," he says. He lifts his glass.

Sarah squints as if the light is suddenly too bright.

"Is this some kind of joke?" she says.

Smiling, Richard shakes his head. "The damndest thing," he says. "But Green says it can happen sometimes."

"For Christ's sake! What!"

Richard grins, enjoying himself.

"What!" says Sarah, her voice shaking. "Stop torturing me!"

Richard takes a deep breath. He smiles. "It's gone."

Sarah stares at him. "Remission?"

Richard shakes his head. "All gone. Everywhere. There's not a trace. Not in the brain. Nothing in the blood. She's in the clear. Some kind of minor miracle."

"Minor?" says Sarah. "Minor! My God! I can't believe it!"

She turns to Mary Beth, frowning.

"Bethie," she says, slowly. "You know what I thought, don't you?"

Mary Beth doesn't answer. She looks past Sarah, out the window.

"Maybe she can't believe it either," says Richard.

"You knew what I was going through," says Sarah. "Why didn't you tell me?"

Mary Beth shrugs.

"You let me worry all afternoon," says Sarah.

Mary Beth hears the anger in her voice.

"I don't understand you, Bethie. I really don't."

She turns away.

Mary Beth looks out the window. There are no lights. No cars pass, and though Sarah says the stars are shining, Mary Beth can't see them. All she sees is night.

Sinners

The moment Ruthie saw the two little Penningtons she knew Jesus had sent her to the right place. In all her years of caring for children, she'd never seen any as needy as these. The boy at least had some color in his cheeks, but the girl's face was pale as chalk and her eyes held that same look of empty sadness that Ruthie remembered in the eyes of certain children down home—half-starving children who never got enough to eat. Only it wasn't food the girl was starving for; Ruthie had seen enough already to know that!

She knelt right down in front of them. "Hello there," she said softly. They sat side by side on the brown sofa, staring at her. The boy blinked. The girl plucked at her dress.

"Dinah! William!" Mrs. Pennington's voice was sharp as glass, but her face softened when she looked at William, and Ruthie knew why Dinah looked the way she did.

"Now I don't mind a bit," she said, smiling at the children as she talked. "They don't even know me yet. If you let us have some time alone, we'll be just fine."

She kept smiling until she heard the mother leave the room, and then she stood and looked around. Mrs. Pennington was gone, but the smell of perfumed scent and stale tobacco lay heavy in the stuffy air.

"First things first," said Ruthie, and she walked right over to the windows. "Good clean air just going to waste! All that sun and all that snow. Like frosting on a birthday cake."

She was a big strong woman but it seemed like these windows had been glued shut and never opened. She tugged and tugged, feeling the sweat collect beneath her dress, but all the while she kept on talking, letting the words out slow and easy.

"Oh my! Looks like your other sitters weren't raised on a farm the way I was. Didn't know how good that winter air can smell. Why, every winter day, my Daddy and me, we'd be out there chopping wood. Oh, I could chop all day and not get tired, and my Daddy used to say, 'Ruthie, if you aren't the strongest worker I ever did see!'" She chuckled as the window came up half an inch, and right away she moved on to the next. "That's what he said all right. Oh, there was work. Had to be with all those mouths to feed, but there was plenty of time for fun. You can bet I have some stories about that!" She moved right down the row of windows, each one lifting easier than the one before. When she was done, she turned, smiling, to the children. "Open up your hearts and let the sun shine in," she sang softly so as not to frighten them.

The children didn't say a word. They stared, and so did Ruthie. "If you aren't the prettiest," she said, smiling. It was the truth. They were the prettiest children she had ever seen.

William was plump and rosy with blond hair and eyes the color of forget-me-nots. Dinah's hair was dark and shiny, and her pale skin made Ruthie think of cream. Pale as cream and smooth as petals, and Ruthie longed to touch it. But it was too soon for that so instead she knelt back down, and smiled up into their faces.

"Well, now," she said, "I hear you've had sitters turning over faster than hotcakes on a griddle, but you'd better know you won't be getting rid of Ruthie so fast. No, siree. Old Ruthie is here to stay, and I tell you we're going to have some fun!"

"Fun," said William in a small hoarse voice.

"That's what I said, honey. You just wait and see."

"He always does that," said Dinah.

"What's that, sweetheart?"

"He's not saying anything. He just repeats the last word. Like a baby."

"A baby!" said Ruthie. She smiled at William. "Why, I heard you were four years old. Much too big to be a baby!"

"Baby," said William, and then he smiled.

"See?" said Dinah, smug.

Ruthie turned to smile at her. "You know what I see, honey," she said. "Two children I just now met and already I feel a whole lot of love."

"I'm not little," said Dinah. "I'm nine years old already!"

"I know that," Ruthie said, "and I know something else." Leaning closer, she touched her finger to Dinah's knee. Dinah blinked, but didn't pull away. "I know those two little children are going to learn to love me back."

Dinah didn't answer, but Ruthie felt a shivering in Dinah's skin, and she praised the power of His love.

Later the children showed her through the house. It was all one floor, long and narrow like a coffin, with the children living at one end and the parents at the other. The parents both worked, and there was money; Ruthie could see that right away. But for all the money there was nothing pretty anywhere, just bare white walls and plate glass windows and rugs like burlap on the floors.

They found the parents in the library, and Mr. Pennington stood up the minute Ruthie came through the door, a big man, blond and beefy with a look in his eye and a hard strong handshake. "Wonderful!" He squeezed her fingers. "Welcome aboard."

He kept hold of her hand as if he'd forgotten that his wife was there, and Ruthie had to pull away.

"A sight for sore eyes," he said, grinning, staring right at Ruthie's dress.

Ruthie heard Mrs. Pennington sigh. She looked at her, her sharp face and legs like pole beans in tight brown pants, and though she knew the husband for a sinner she felt sorry for him all the same. Like her daddy always said, men like women with some flesh to them, and Mrs. Pennington was nothing much but bone.

"That is one flashy dress!" said Mr. Pennington.

"John," his wife said in a tired voice.

"I'll change into my uniform as soon as I unpack," said Ruthie, but Mrs. Pennington shook her head.

"Only if you want," she said.

Mr. Pennington chuckled. "Absolutely not. Pink and purple. That's quite a combination!" He winked at Ruthie. "We could do with some color in the house," he said, and sinner though he was, Ruthie certainly agreed with that.

Ruthie loved color—she always had—and in this house she was especially glad she didn't have to dress in white. In this house the brightness of her clothes brought comfort, and she walked down dark halls feeling like a beacon. A burning flame.

All the same it wasn't enough.

With her first paycheck she went right out and bought a soft canary-colored rug to place over the brown one in her room.

"Sunlight on the floor," she said to the children who stood, watching, in the doorway. "Come feel." She stood ankle deep in the yellow shag as the children crept closer. "There," she said. She wiggled her toes. "Doesn't that feel good!"

William giggled. "Tickles," he said, and Dinah bent to stroke it with her hands. "Can we lie down?"

"Of course you can, honey. That's what it's for."

So Dinah did, smiling shyly up at Ruthie, who smiled too.

"Aren't you a sight," she said. "Just like you're lying in yellow grass. Reminds me of the hill back home behind the house. That hill had the softest grass you ever felt. Like rolling down from Heaven on a cloud."

"Me too!" said William, trying to push Dinah to one side.

"I got here first!"

"There's room for both," said Ruthie. "I made sure of that." She waited till they were settled side by side. "Don't you look snug," she said. "We used to sleep like that, all cozied up, four to a bed, and my, how we used to carry on with Mama yelling to shut us up." Ruthie chuckled. "Can't say it did much good."

"My mother never yells," said Dinah.

"Nothing wrong with yelling, honey, long as it's done with love. Oh my, we did have fun." Remembering, she shook her head.

"I wish we could have fun like that," said Dinah in a wistful voice.

"I told you we would, the first day I came."

Dinah looked at Ruthie. "My parents have fun," she said.

"I wouldn't know," said Ruthie. Stiff.

"They do," said Dinah. She sat up. "I hear them, all the time. Last night when I got up to go I heard them dancing in the hall. I saw them too. Daddy was dancing with Mrs. Ryan and her pearl necklace popped all over the floor. They laughed and laughed, and then Daddy started crawling on. . . ."

"That's not fun," said Ruthie, and Dinah looked at her, surprised.

"But they were laughing."

"That's sin, child," and Dinah's eyes grew wide.

"You mean bad?"

"That's what I mean," said Ruthie, nodding.

"It's not!" said Dinah. "It's just being silly."

Ruthie shook her head. "The Devil, child. He sneaks inside, and tempts. Drinking, dancing, playing with cards. The Devil's own fun."

Dinah clapped her hand over her mouth as if to keep the Devil out, and Ruthie smiled.

"No need to worry, child. The Devil won't trouble you. You've got me and you've got Jesus. The whole world knows that He loves little children best."

"I'm not little!" said Dinah, scowling.

"You're little enough," said Ruthie, "to have Jesus keep you safe." She smiled at her. "Now who's going to brush my hair today?"

"Me!" said William, shouting like he always did.

"Me," said Dinah in a whisper, and when Ruthie held the brush toward her, Dinah shyly took it.

Ruthie settled on the yellow rug as Dinah edged around her, brushing so lightly that Ruthie could hardly feel the strokes. Still, in four weeks it was the first time Dinah had touched her of her own accord, which wasn't any wonder considering how little love was in the child's life. A string of sitters and two parents working in the city all day, but even at night Ruthie couldn't see they did much good. Mrs. Pennington, when she kissed the girl good night, puckered up her lips like she was tasting persimmon, and Mr. Pennington's idea of fun was to toss her up into the air until she screamed with terror.

Ruthie sat stark still so as not to startle her, and slowly Dinah's strokes got stronger. Ruthie closed her eyes and sighed with pleasure. "Harder, child. You can't hurt me!" And Dinah brushed harder until Ruthie's scalp tingled and her skin went tight. "Oh my," she said.

"That does feel good! It's been a long time since anybody's brushed my hair. My daddy now, he used to do the brushing when I was young. My hair was so long and thick, he was the only one could get clear to the bottom."

"It's still thick," said Dinah.

"Oh, honey. Not like then. Then it used to go right down to my waist. Oh, it was pretty hair, I have to say."

"It's still pretty," said Dinah, shyly.

"Dinah Pennington. Don't you know how to make an old lady feel good!"

"You're not old," said Dinah, and smiling, Ruthie shook her head.

"Forty in the summer, child, and that sounds old enough to me."

"You're young," said Dinah. "You're pretty too!"

And Ruthie laughed.

"It's love," she said. "It's love makes people pretty and I'm just bursting with it." She opened her eyes and smiled at Dinah. "It's time," she said. "Let's have some fun!"

She took the children into the playroom, where she sat down at the old upright by the windows and began to play. She played by ear, "Love of Jesus, Light the Way," singing along as loud as she could, her foot tapping and her body swaying, and sure enough by the time she reached the last verse, she heard Dinah humming, right on tune. Ruthie never stopped but swung into "This World Is Not My Home," and after that "Give Me Oil in My Lamp." By the time she got to "I've Got a Mansion," Dinah was singing right along in a high sweet voice, and Ruthie had only to look into her clear bright eyes to see that Jesus was on His way.

It was, however, Mr. Pennington who came first, and just when Ruthie figured she was safe.

One night when she was at the piano, the children too, all dressed for bed and all three singing, Ruthie smelled him coming, smelled whiskey and tobacco coming through the door. She kept on playing, though he came to stand so close behind she felt his breath on her bare neck, felt goose bumps rising on her arms. Thinking on Jesus to steady herself, she played through right to the end, and when she stopped, he touched her shoulder.

"Fantastic!" he said. "A real disco beat."

"Gospel," said Ruthie, standing fast.

"Dancing's a sin, Daddy," Dinah said, and her father laughed.

"Good God!" he said. "Who told you that?"

"Ruthie did. She says. . . ."

Ruthie clapped her hands. "Bedtime," she said, her voice so sharp that Dinah stared, then scuttled sideways out the door.

Ruthie would have left right then, but Mr. Pennington was in the way, leaning close, and grinning with his whiskey breath.

"You're doing a great job, Ruthie," he said. "I just wanted to tell you that."

"They're easy to love," said Ruthie, stiff as she could. She felt her skin burn where his hand had touched her.

"Maybe," said Mr. Pennington. "But all the same you've got a way with kids. I'm surprised you never had some of your own. Matter of fact . . . ." He cocked his head, teeth gleaming when he smiled. "I'm surprised you never married."

"I'm married all right," said Ruthie, tossing her head so her hair swung from side to side, and to her satisfaction she saw Mr. Pennington look surprised. She smiled right into his flirting eyes. "To Jesus," she said. And before he could say another word, she walked past him, down the hall.

That night her sleep was troubled, so troubled that at three she got down on her knees to pray. Night was the Devil's own time, the way he had of sneaking into dreams. That night she dreamt of Mr. Pennington, his white teeth, his clean strong hands. In the dream he picked up Ruthie's hairbrush, picked it up in such a way that at first she thought he meant to strike her. But no, instead he started to brush her hair, the strokes so hard that her whole body began to sway. "How's that, Ruthie? That feel good?" asked Mr. Pennington in her daddy's voice, just the way her daddy had, and Ruthie woke fast, her heart beating like a bird's, and got down quickly on her knees.

On her knees she prayed to Jesus, thanked Him for her saving so many years ago, but hard as she prayed she couldn't stop the pictures rising, pictures of Ruthie as a child. Ruthie and her daddy, fishing. The still brown pond, the lacy willow on the bank, and nothing moving except a dragonfly with rainbow wings, and her daddy and her daddy's hands. That feel good, Ruthie? That feel good? Ruthie and her daddy all alone, the rod propped on a willow root and the red cork bobbing and the bees humming in the meadow, a soft hum tight beneath her skin.

Ruthie got up. Nighttime was trouble, and sometimes even praying didn't help. She turned on the light, and sitting on the bed she brushed her hair, one hundred strokes and then one hundred strokes again. Oh, she was not without sin: she knew that, knew her hair was her pride, her body too. But married to Jesus she was safe.

Morning was Ruthie's favorite time. Darkness was the Devil's own, but morning brought comfort, especially when the children took to creeping into her room before she was awake. Giggling and whispering, they'd climb into her bed and snuggle down, their small pure bodies like summer flowers against her skin.

It seemed to Ruthie that Dinah took to cuddling more than any child she'd ever known. Now that she was no longer scared, she was always leaning close, holding Ruthie's hand, even sitting on her lap. It was as if after years of starving she was finally getting enough to eat. Her dark eyes, so like her mother's, took on a shine, and her pale face turned pink. Now, instead of scooting sideways, she ran straight for Ruthie and leapt, laughing, into her arms.

The days grew longer, the air like honey, and Ruthie, knowing what spring could do, worried that Mr. Pennington might come again. One soft night the parents gave a party on the lawn, and after the children were asleep, Ruthie stood by the window, peeking out. There were colored lanterns hanging from the trees, and if it hadn't been for the sin that light revealed it would have been a pretty sight. She saw Mr. Pennington dancing with some red-haired woman, dancing close, saw his shirt wide open at the neck. She leaned out to get a better look, and just then Mr. Pennington turned and waved. Quickly Ruthie ducked back in, but not before she saw him whisper to the woman, heard them laugh. Her heart ached. Sinners, she thought, knowing they would burn in Hell.

With the weather fine now, she went out with the children every day. Beyond the garden was a small pond with a mossy bank and lily pads and two white swans. The moss was soft, and Ruthie lay still, feeling the sun push hot against her skin. Dinah mostly lay beside her, their arms touching, while William played. In the hot sun, William peeled pink but Dinah's skin turned brown like Ruthie's. The exact same color.

"Toast color," Dinah said.

"Butterscotch," said Ruthie, and Dinah laid her cheek on Ruthie's arm.

"Maybe you're my real mother," she said, and Ruthie heard her hoping it was so.

"I'm not that," said Ruthie, "but I love you like a real mother."

"I don't think that's very much," said Dinah, and gently Ruthie stroked her hair.

"There's love and love," she said, "but remember, child, Jesus' love is best."

Dinah sat up, one strap of her sundress sliding down, and Ruthie tugged it back in place.

"Ruthie," said Dinah, "is it true you're married to Jesus?"

"It surely is."

"Is that why Daddy calls you a Jesus freak?"

Ruthie sighed. "Your daddy doesn't know what he's saying."

"He says you're asking for it. I heard him telling Mommy that. But I don't know what that means."

"That means that men can be the Devil sometimes. That's the Devil speaking." And taking Dinah by the shoulders, she looked her in the eyes. "You listen, child. It's Jesus who saves. I wasn't much older than you when Jesus found me, took me for His own. It was He who saved me from temptation."

"What's that?" asked Dinah.

"Wanting to do what's bad."

"Why would they?"

"Because it feels good. That's why."

Dinah looked where Ruthie's hand was on her shoulder. She looked at Ruthie, and Ruthie saw the worry in her eyes. "It feels good when you touch me, Ruthie. Is that bad?"

Laughing, Ruthie hugged her. "Course not, honey. There's touching and there's touching, just like there're different kinds of love. But you just wait till Jesus touches. You feel Jesus, you'll be saved!"

"Saved!" said William, and Ruthie turned quickly, hoping, but William grinned, and she knew it was only his old trick of repeating words. Gently she touched her face. "Never mind, angel. Jesus is coming to you too."

All summer Ruthie waited for His coming. August came and still there hadn't been a Sign. In August Dinah would be ten and Ruthie forty. She'd been with them seven months, and in that time Dinah had grown an inch. Her kneecaps, so bony when Ruthie had arrived, were round and smooth. Her legs were long, and she had a way of cocking her head that made Ruthie think of Mr. Pennington.

She was too big now for her father to toss into the air. Instead he lifted her, big as she was, and carried her down the hall to greet the guests, leaving Ruthie to watch them go. Watching, she saw the light in Dinah's eyes, and though she knew herself the joy of being a daddy's favorite, she also knew that time was running short.

Ruthie's birthday came first, and just as the sky was turning pink the children leapt into her room, Dinah holding a small wrapped present in her hand. "It's breakable," she said, so excited she could not stay still. She hopped, from one foot to the other as Ruthie pulled off the paper and opened the box to find Jesus in a gilt frame, smiling.

"If you aren't the smartest!" she said, giving her a great big hug. "Exactly what I wanted most!"

And Dinah nodded, shy and pleased. "You know how you say he's your best friend? Well, everyone wants pictures of their best friend!"

"They sure do," said Ruthie. Hugging Dinah, she held her close. "And do you know He's your best friend too?"

"If he's yours," said Dinah, "then he's mine!" And Ruthie felt Him coming closer.

Dinah's birthday was four days later. "Double digits," her mother said. "As a special treat you can stay up late and eat with us."

Dinah was excited. Too excited. Ruthie had to speak sharply to calm her down. Just before she went off down the hall, Ruthie handed her her present. Inside a real jeweler's box lined with blue satin was a small gold cross on a thin gold chain. Dinah's face flushed with pleasure at the sight.

"Can I wear it now?" she said, and, smiling, Ruthie fastened the chain around her neck, then tucked the cross inside her dress, making sure it was concealed. "There," she said, "this way Jesus is right next to your heart."

After she'd gone, it seemed so quiet. William sat, lonesome on the sofa, sucking his thumb. Ruthie, to distract him, played some gospel on the piano. It was a hot still night and her fingers kept sticking to the keys. William came over to sit beside her, but he was sticky too and his off-key croak was jangling to her nerves.

At eight she put him to bed, and then she settled down for prayer. Usually praying was like falling into trance; she could slip so deep inside herself that all but Jesus was forgotten.

But not tonight. It was so hot. Her hair felt heavy, damp and prickly on her neck. A mosquito kept buzzing in her ear, and even on the soft shag her knees were aching. Every few minutes she opened her eyes to look at the clock, watching the hands inch slowly toward nine, but still there was no sign of Dinah.

At nine-fifteen Ruthie got up off her knees. Birthday or not, it was time for little girls to be in bed. She got up and marched down the long hall toward the dining room. She heard moths banging against the screens, saw shadows growing on the walls. Ruthie marched right into the dining room.

And there she stopped.

The room was lit by candles, which made it difficult to see, but even so, she saw enough. She saw the three of them, grouped at one end of the long dark table, Mrs. Pennington beside her husband, and Dinah sitting on his lap. She saw smoke from their cigarettes drift toward the candle flames, and red wine gleaming in three crystal glasses, and Dinah leaning back against her father, her eyes half-closed, his arms tight around her waist.

"Ruthie," she said in a sleepy voice, and smiled.

"Ruthie!" said Mr. Pennington. "Just in time to toast our grown-up girl."

"Ten always was my favorite age," said Mrs. Pennington. Sipping her wine, she smiled at Ruthie.

But Ruthie didn't smile.

"It's Dinah's bedtime."

Mr. Pennington only laughed. "If looks could kill," he said.

"That child is too young for wine and too old to be sitting in her daddy's lap," said Ruthie.

"I'm having fun" said Dinah. "Please!"

"Now!" said Ruthie.

"Don't be a spoilsport," said Mr. Pennington as Ruthie bent and, taking Dinah by the shoulders, pulled.

"Ouch," said Dinah. "Don't. That hurts!"

"Let go of her," said Ruthie.

"For Christ's sake!" said Mr. Pennington, holding Dinah all the tighter.

He held on and Ruthie tugged and Dinah's eyes filled up with tears.

"Stop," she whimpered.

"Jesus!" said Mr. Pennington. "What the hell is going on?"

"You ought to be ashamed!" said Ruthie.

"Of what!"

"John," murmured Mrs. Pennington.

"Well, what's she think? I'm going to rape her?"

"Sinner!" cried Ruthie. "Let go!"

"Jesus Christ!" he said. And he let go. "I told you she was asking for it."

"John," said Mrs. Pennington.

But Ruthie pretended not to hear.

Without another word, she marched Dinah down the hall and into bed, and then she went to bed herself. Only she couldn't sleep. She couldn't stop those pictures rising, and all night she tossed and turned, and in the morning she sat the children down and told them about Hell.

Hell, she said, looking at Dinah as she talked, was for those who spent time carrying on, staying up late and drinking.

"I didn't drink!" said Dinah. "I tasted it, and it was yucky."

But Ruthie wasn't going to listen. She told them about the vats of burning oil and heavy chains folks had to wear, each link another sin. She told them those too blind to see the Light had eyes poked out with burning needles. There was no love in Hell, she said, and nothing pretty, just grief and pain. She kept right on until William's lips began to tremble and he burst into tears. "No more," said William, sobbing, but Dinah sat sullen, hard as stone, picking on her fingernails.

"I didn't sin. I know I didn't."

"There's sin and sin," said Ruthie, scooping William up to comfort.

"It was fun!" said Dinah. "The best birthday I ever had."

"Just like there's different kinds of fun. Good clean fun and the Devil's own and Jesus waiting to save you too!"

"I don't need Jesus, Ruthie. I have you."

"Not without Jesus," Ruthie said.

Dinah looked at her, eyes going wide.

"Don't leave me, Ruthie!" she cried, jumping up and throwing her arms around Ruthie's neck. "Don't, Ruthie. Please!"

Ruthie gave her back a pat. "Now I never said I would. Don't worry, child. Repent your sins, and you'll have me and Jesus both."

And sure enough it was that very night that Jesus chose to come. Some time after midnight Ruthie woke, hearing crying from William's room. She found him sitting up in bed, tears streaming fast. He stretched his arms to Ruthie. "Saved, Ruthie, saved."

"Glory be!" cried Ruthie, and dropping to her knees, she prayed. They prayed together, William on his knees beside her, repeating after her the sins he chose to leave behind forever.

It wasn't till they were done, and Ruthie was helping him back to bed, that she saw Dinah, scowling, in the doorway.

"He had a nightmare," she said. "He's not saved. A great big baby, scared of Hell."

"You hush!" said Ruthie.

"I won't. He just wants you to love him best."

Ruthie patted William's head. "I love both of you and Jesus too."

"Stupid Jesus," muttered Dinah.

"Jesus!" said William. "Baby Jesus."

"Shut up, baby!" Dinah, fists clenched, moved toward him but Ruthie moved faster, and grabbing her shoulders, shook her hard, trying to shake the Devil out.

In the morning only William climbed into Ruthie's bed, and together they snuggled down to pray. It was only later, when they were up and dressed, that Dinah appeared, standing in the doorway, still in her nightgown, her long legs bare.

"Ruthie," she whispered. "I've been saved."

"Look at me, child," Ruthie said, and when Dinah did, Ruthie saw her cold dark eyes.

"Jesus doesn't like liars," said Ruthie, spacing the words so they fell like stones, and after one quick awful look, Dinah ran to her bedroom and slammed the door.

All day she acted like the Devil was in her. When William built a tower with blocks, she waited until the last block was set on top, then knocked it down. When William cried, she laughed, pulling her eyes into slits and sticking out her tongue. At the pond she threw stones at the swans until they hissed with rage, beating the water with their wings, and William, frightened, cried again. "Crybaby!" Dinah sneered, and Ruthie sent her to the house. She went slowly, not looking back, kicking at pebbles on the path.

When William and Ruthie came up from the pond, she was playing slapjack on the playroom floor. "Want to play?" she asked William, and Ruthie had to hold him back.

"You've been saved, honey. Remember that."

"Stupid saving!" said Dinah, slapping so hard the windows rattled, and Ruthie's heart began to ache.

She crouched down next to Dinah. "Jesus loves you, sweetheart." She touched Dinah's shoulder. "And I do too. You do know that?"

"There's love and love," said Dinah in a hard flat voice, and Ruthie felt a sharp pain in her heart.

"Sweet Jesus," Ruthie prayed that night. "Save Dinah as You once saved me!" But her heart was heavy and her dreams were bad. In one dream Jesus came, His white robes rustling as He bent to kiss. "There's love and love," He said in her daddy's voice, His hot breath trembling on her neck so that when Ruthie woke she trembled too, woke, worrying that Dinah might be right.

Waking, she heard drums beating and horns wailing like cats in heat. She thought at first she might be dreaming, but the sky was pink and the music, loud enough to dance her skin, was coming from the other room.

She climbed quickly out of bed. When she opened the door, her heart stopped beating.

Dinah was dancing, swaying around William, who sat wide-eyed on the floor. "Temptation, I am Temptation," sang Dinah in her high clear voice. In one hand she held a pack of cards, and the other was pressed against her chest, against her thin white nightie through which her naked body was revealed.

She stretched her hand toward her brother. "Come," she sang, "have fun with me," and William, giggling, started to rise.

"Shame!" shouted Ruthie so loud that both children turned to stare, and Dinah's arms dropped to her sides. There was the small sound of splintering glass, and looking, Ruthie saw Jesus, the gilt frame broken, lying in pieces on the floor. She looked at Dinah as the music played, saw the gold cross shimmering on her neck.

"Dancing with Jesus!" she said in such a voice that Dinah's face turned pale.

"I was lonely, Ruthie," Dinah whispered, looking so stricken, so lost and little that, for one moment, Ruthie was tempted to forgive.

Skinner

Nineteen! Biggest litter he ever had. Skinner can't get over it. He counts again. So far they all look healthy, too. He shakes his head.

Skinner steps out of the farrowing shed, and first thing he sees is his wife, down by their mailbox on the county road. Her blue parka is flapping in the wind, but she's just standing, holding a letter in her hand. She hasn't opened it; she doesn't have to. Skinner can tell from the angle of her head that she knows as well as he does what it is.

He turns fast, before she sees him, and walks behind the shed, past the old shed, past the barn. Past the boar pen. He hears the boars shoving up against the fence, shoving hard, grunting, wanting to be fed. The fence post creaks. But Skinner's fed them once already. He's fed them all, all seven hundred, fed and watered in the morning. By nine o'clock. In twelve years he has yet to miss a single day.

The gilts, seeing him coming, push up against their fences too, but Skinner walks right past them and heads across the fields toward the slough.

Overhead the sky is gray and the fields are empty, except for mud. Minnesota mud. Only mud that Skinner's ever known. Flat fields and sky. Skinner could see to South Dakota if he wanted. He doesn't. The farmhouse is behind him, but Skinner doesn't look. When he hears the school bus coming, he walks faster. He hears the mud sucking at his boots. He sees a fence along the soybean field that needs repairing. He walks as fast as the thick March mud will let him.

The slough looks dirty, filled with rotting ice. He sees dead branches, an old fence post, floating. Two ducks, mallards, paddle along the edge. By his feet lies an old pail Skinner remembers using as a child. But maybe not. Skinner is thirty-five. Maybe he dropped it here himself not long ago. He picks it up. The sides are dented, and the bottom rusted with a hole or two. The handle holds though.

Skinner holds it. He looks down into the slough. The snow has melted from the sloping sides. He sees the bones of dead pigs poking through the mud. His dad used the slough as a graveyard too. What they don't know won't hurt them, he used to say.

Squinting, Skinner narrows his eyes. The white bones look like spears. The mallards waddle across the mud, their orange feet as bright as Skinner's hunting cap. If Skinner had his gun along, he'd shoot them. He just might even though the season's past.

Squinting, his eyes begin to water. He rubs them hard. Even in March that wind sweeping down from Canada is cold.

He walks back to the farrowing shed and slips inside. His boots are caked with mud, and heavy. He kicks them off. He washes his hands with disinfectant, staring at the syringes above the sink. He remembers five years ago when this shed was new. He's hardly lost a pig since then. His dad now, he'd lose twenty at a time from scours. Since Skinner had the water fixed he hasn't had one case of scours.

He hears sows grunting, their litters squealing. Opening the second door, he steps inside. He sees that, somehow, he's still got that old pail in his hand.

Skinner's done the pigs already. He's done his chores. Just the same he does them all again. He doesn't use the belt for feeding. Instead he feeds them just the way he used to. He takes that old pail to the bin and fills it, using his hands to scoop. Skinner has big hands. They hold a lot.

He walks down the aisle between the pens, filling troughs already full. Some sows are eating, some lying on their sides to let their litters nurse. Skinner saves the latest litter for last. He counts again, just making sure. He wonders why they had to come today.

He hears the shed door open, but Skinner doesn't look. He knows who's there. He hears his breathing. Slow steady breathing. Like Skinner's. The boy moves closer.

"She had them?"

Skinner keeps his head down, counting. One, two, three. The boy moves close to Skinner.

"How many?" he says. He starts breathing faster. Excited.

But Skinner doesn't look. He doesn't turn around. He knows his wife is standing by the door. Just standing.

Skinner clears his throat. "Nineteen," he says. His voice sounds rusty.

"Gee," says the boy. He leans over to get a better look. His hair swings down, his legs up, leaning his stomach against the gate. His face turns red. "Awesome!" he says, his voice scratchy because of the gate against his stomach. Skinner takes hold of his jacket collar and pulls him up.

"You watch out!" says Skinner. Rough.

The boy looks at him.

Skinner turns to his wife. She just stands there, looking at Skinner with her big dark eyes, eyes like the boy's.

"Hon," she says.

"Don't tell me," Skinner says. "I already know."

Skinner knows. Only he's not sure how it happened. How any of it happened. Or why.

He does know this: it was his wife who named him Skinner, in the Cities twelve years ago, at the apartment of a friend.

"What's your name?" she said, her voice hard to hear with all the noise, in the room and on the street. It was spring, the windows open, and all around the sound of cars and trucks and people. Whenever he thinks of cities now, he thinks of noise.

She stood right next to him, a city girl he'd never met before that night.

"Skinny," he said, blushing. He grinned, awkward, shifting a beer from hand to hand. She was drinking rum and coke.

"Skinny!" she said. She looked him up and down. "A great big man like you!"

The way she said it made Skinner feel bigger. She smiled. Her name was Tamsin, a name Skinner had never heard before. It made him think of flowers. She was a big girl, big and easy, and the way she moved made Skinner think of wheat in wind. Blushing when he told her that, afraid she wouldn't like it. There were girls back home who wouldn't like it, but Tamsin laughed.

"That's nice," she said. "That's real nice."

Which made Skinner blush some more. She looked him up and down and Skinner saw that she was thinking, only he didn't know just what. And then she nodded.

"Skinner," she said. "That suits you better."

"How come?" said Skinner, feeling strong.

"Foxy," said Tamsin. "A foxy name. Like you."

There are still times when Skinner wonders how it happened. Someone loving him enough to marry him. Times when it seems like some kind of miracle. Like now.

"Guess I better finish up in here," says Skinner.

His wife looks around the shed, seeing that he's already done his chores. But she doesn't say. She nods.

"Okay," she says. She looks at the boy who's still looking at the pigs. "You too," she says. "You leave your dad alone."

The boy turns, looking up at Skinner with his big brown eyes. His mother's eyes.

"I want to stay," he says.

When this boy looks at you he sees you, not like the others, not like his older brother. Now that boy, his eyes never stop. He'll look at you, but he's not seeing you. He's seeing something a million miles away. Bookish, that one, and Skinner is proud of him. He guesses his wife is that much prouder. She thinks he'll be a teacher maybe. But not this one, with the brown eyes. Staring.

Skinner feels a hand close on his heart.

"You heard your mama," he says, louder than he means to.

The boy goes slowly, not looking back. Skinner's heart hurts so bad it's hard to breathe. He sees the old pail, empty now, grain leaking from the bottom, setting by his feet. He picks it up and hurls it against the wall.

Skinner's always known that bad news travels fast.

Just two days later he's sitting in the living room. Just sitting. Sitting on the red couch and staring at his hands. Opening and closing his hands. Doing nothing except watching his hands do nothing too.

The baby's in the playpen, and the oldest, he's got his head hidden behind a book. The others are walking around the living room. Quiet. Waiting for supper. The TV's on, but no one's watching. They're watching him.

The girl comes close. Skinner feels her standing there. He doesn't look. He looks at his hands. He hears his wife behind him, cooking supper on the stove. He hears grease hissing on the griddle. Pancakes, he thinks. He turns, sees tears falling, falling from her eyes onto the griddle. Her tears hissing. Her head is down. Skinner turns back quickly before she sees him looking. The kids are staring. At him. Skinner stares at his hands.

"I did everything I could," he says.

The baby drops his rattle on the floor. He starts to cry.

"I know that," says his wife.

The phone rings.

"You get that for me," says his wife, so Skinner does.

It's Skinner's sister, his baby sister, calling from the Cities.

"I just heard," she says. "It was like someone stuck a knife in me. I guess you know as well as anyone how long that farm's been in the family?"

"I guess I do," says Skinner.

"One hundred years!" his sister says.

"I guess I know that," Skinner says.

The baby's crying makes it hard to hear.

"I keep thinking," says his sister. "If only you hadn't built that shed. One hundred and fifty thousand dollars just thrown away."

"It wasn't just that," says Skinner.

"You're telling me!" his sister says. "There was that quarter section you bought from Larsen. I never could see why you did that when you could hardly manage what you got."

"Well," says Skinner. "I just did is all."

He holds his big hand over the phone. "Could someone shut that baby up?"

"You still there?" says his sister.

"I'm here," says Skinner.

His girl picks up the rattle from the floor and puts it in the baby's hand. The crying stops. He remembers when his sister was the same size as his little girl.

"The time I did it, all those things," he says, "FHA was telling us they were good things to do."

"Now," says his sister, "I suppose you're blaming them?"

He remembers how she used to climb into his bed at night to warm her feet.

"I'm not blaming anyone," he says.

"Things don't happen for no reason," says his sister.

"Maybe," says Skinner. "Only I just don't see what else I could have done."

"Who was that?" his wife says, looking at the griddle, not at him.

"Debbie," says Skinner, "calling from the Cities." He looks at the griddle too, watches the bubbles rising in the batter. Behind him the baby starts to cry.

"What'd she want?" says his wife.

"Oh," says Skinner. "She'd heard the news is all. Just called to say how sorry she was."

His wife glances at him. Skinner sees how the heat has curled her hair, tight curls sticking to her forehead. Curls shaped like little hearts.

"I bet," she says.

Skinner turns away, walks over to the baby. He picks him up. Skinner's hands are big, meeting around the baby's middle. The baby stops crying. He looks at Skinner with his big round eyes. "Dada," he says. Skinner holds him up against his face to smell his skin. The baby laughs. Skinner spins him so that he's hanging upside down. His feet kick. His face turns red. Looking at the world from upside down, he laughs and laughs. Skinner wonders what the world looks like upside down. He guesses he knows.

"We have to," says Skinner. "We have to eat."

His wife is angry. He's never seen her quite so angry. Her face is red, bright red except for the dark circles under her eyes. She stuffs the baby in the snowsuit, stuffing hard, like she was shoving potatoes in a sack.

"We don't have to do anything we don't want!"

Skinner looks at his hands. "Eat," he says.

"Nobody can make us," she says. "You know how it's going to be. Standing in that line, everyone knowing why I'm there!"

Skinner doesn't look at her. He looks at his hands.

"We got the kids to think of," he says.

"Well, maybe," she says, breathing hard, the way she does when she gets mad, "Well maybe Mr. Skinner know-it-all, we should have thought of them before!"

When she comes back, she finds Skinner in the shed. "Oh, hon," she says. "I'm sorry."

Skinner is shoveling grain from bin to bin. He keeps on shoveling. His hands feel easy on the shovel.

"I brought you out here," he says. "You never liked the pigs much anyway."

"It's not that," his wife says. "It's just I get so angry. I don't know what to do with all this anger." Her voice comes closer. "Skinner," she says, "how come you're not angry? You ought to be out there killing folks."

Skinner stops shoveling. "Who?" he says. He looks at her. She's standing close now, holding a bag of groceries in her arms. The bag says SEASONS GREETINGS, and for a minute Skinner gets confused; maybe it's still just Christmas, and he's been dreaming.

She sees him looking. "They had a surplus," his wife says.

Skinner looks at her.

"I keep wondering," he says, "what it is that I've done wrong."

"Oh, hon!" She drops the bag, and Skinner hears glass breaking on the floor. All around them pigs are squealing. She leans against him.

"I love you," she says. "You put your arms around me."

Skinner does, even though he's wearing piggy clothes. She's always hated piggy clothes.

"I'm kind of piggy," he says.

"I don't care what you are," his wife says. "I love you anyway." She looks up, and Skinner sees her eyes are red. She must have been crying all the way into town, and out.

"I'll tell you something funny," she says. "You know how mad I was about those food stamps. Thinking how everyone would know?"

"That's right," says Skinner.

"You were right," his wife says. "It didn't matter how it made me feel. We had to. For the food. For the kids."

She steps away from Skinner, and points down to the bag of groceries on the floor. The bag is ripped, wet with juices leaking through. "That's it," she says. "That's all we got. One bag. Twenty dollars' worth a month." She looks at Skinner and shakes her head. "All that worrying I did for nothing," she says. She laughs.

Skinner knows she's waiting for him to laugh too. So Skinner does; but what he wants to do is cry.

He does cry when the semi pulls up the driveway for the pigs. Not right away though. He sees the boy watching, standing by the farrowing shed. The other kids are watching from the house. Skinner doesn't have to turn to know. He feels them watching. His wife too.

Two men climb out of the semi and open up the back. Inside Skinner sees a big black hole.

"I'm real sorry about this," says one.

Skinner shrugs. "These things happen, I guess," he says.

The man spits sideways, into the mud. "I guess," he says.

They go into the shed. The boy stands, watching Skinner.

"You're not going to *let* them, are you?" he says.

His eyes go right through Skinner. Skinner starts to bleed inside.

"You get out of here," says Skinner. The boy stands still. He doesn't move. His boots are caked with mud. He holds his hands out like he's praying.

"Won't!" he says.

The men come out, pigs under either arm, small pigs wriggling like pink worms. The men don't look at Skinner or at the boy. They throw the babies in the back, go back for more.

The boy looks at Skinner though. "We never had a litter that big before," he says.

"I mean it," says Skinner. "You go on into the house, in with the others."

That boy, the way his eyes look at Skinner. Big eyes, clear as slough water on a sunny day.

"You said," says the boy. "You said that when I got bigger I could be your partner. You said this was going to be my farm too."

Something squeezes Skinner's heart.

"I didn't," he said. "You got brothers, don't you? It's not just you."

"Liar!" says the boy.

Skinner raises his hand. The boy steps back, his eyes unblinking. In them Skinner sees himself.

"You think I like this?" he says. "You think I'm doing this on purpose?"

The boy blinks tears. "Who cares," he says. "Who wants to be a dumb old farmer anyway?"

Skinner covers his face with his hands. He hears the sound of the boy's boots in the mud, running to the house. He hears the door slam. He hears the men, the squealing pigs.

"Don't suppose you'd like to lend a hand?" says one. "Get it over faster that way."

Skinner shakes his head. Both men have their caps pulled low so they don't have to look at him.

Skinner walks across the farmyard to the machine shed. The shed is big and dark and cold. He smells the grain stored at the back. He looks up at the combine. A John Deere, ten years old. Skinner bought it secondhand, but he's taken care. It runs like new. He guesses it might go for something; but what good is something to him now?

He climbs up the ladder to the cab. Closing the door, he sits behind the wheel. He remembers teaching the boy to drive, holding him on his lap so that he could see above the wheel. That's how small he was. Maybe five or six, and Skinner holding boy and wheel both.

He doesn't hold the wheel now. He holds his hands. He looks at them. Big hands. Like his dad's.

His dad now used to hit him all the time, him and all the others too. There were nine kids, and Skinner, in the middle, the only one who wasn't good at school.

He was Skinny then, not Skinner, but his real name was Sam. A skinny kid with big hands and bigger feet. He moved slow on those big feet, but steady. His hands were steady too. He remembers once his dad saying, "Looks like you got a way with animals all right," remembers how good that made him feel. It made him feel that finally he was doing something right.

Not that it meant his dad wanted him to have the farm. Fact was, of all those kids, Skinner was the only one who wanted it. Just like his boy.

Skinner turns his hands over to see if the backs look different from the fronts. Large hands with square-tipped fingers. Back or front, they look pretty much the same, look like they belong together. His dad's hands, though, they were big and mean. He was always hitting Skinner and the others, but Skinner's never once hit anyone. "You're so good," his wife says. "That's why I love you."

Now look what he's almost gone and done, how close he came to hitting that boy. That boy who has always wanted to be like him.

But what is Skinner now? And what does he have left to give?

Skinner puts his hands up to his face, and sitting in the combine, cries.

Skinner lies awake in bed. Used to be he'd fall asleep the minute his head was on the pillow, used to be he'd sleep right through the night.

He hears his wife beside him; turning in her sleep, he thinks. But she's wakeful too. She touches his cheek. "You want a back rub?" Skinner shakes his head.

"When the auction's over," she says softly, "we can put it all behind us."

Skinner stares up at the ceiling. "When the auction's over," he says, "we won't have nothing left."

"Each other," she says. "The kids. We don't need more than that."

Skinner sits up. His back aches. His whole body aches.

"You tell me," he says. "What am I supposed to be? If I'm not a farmer, you tell me what I am?"

She runs her finger along his arm. "A man," she says. "That's good enough for me."

Skinner gets up, swinging his long legs out of the bed, onto the floor. The floor is cold. His feet hit with a thud. He gets up and goes into the kitchen. He thinks his wife might follow him. She doesn't though.

He doesn't blame her.

He turns on the light and opens the cabinet above the stove. He sees the whiskey bottle behind the flour. He takes it down, and pours two fingers' worth into a plastic glass. He feels the burn as it goes down. He's never liked the taste of whiskey much. He drinks it anyway.

Then Skinner goes into the living room and sits. He just sits, staring at his hands. He tries to think what they can do.

But he can't think. He's too tired, and there's a buzzing in his head, like static on an empty screen.

Skinner just sits. The buzzing's so loud, he doesn't hear the footsteps, but he feels the hand. A small hand resting on his shoulder. Skinner knows that hand, a small hand with square-tipped fingers, like his own.

"I've been thinking," the boy says in a sleepy voice.

"Is that right?" says Skinner. "I hope your thinking's better than mine."

The boy moves around in front of Skinner. He stands between his knees. His hair is going every which way.

"Did your mama send you out here?" says Skinner.

The boy looks straight at Skinner.

"I'm thinking," he says. "Maybe I'll do dairy instead of pigs."

Skinner clears his throat.

"Is that so?" he says.

The boy nods. "I'm thinking," says the boy, "thinking maybe you could help."

Skinner swallows. He swallows hard. There's a big lump there inside.

"Maybe," he says.

He lifts his hand and lays it on the boy's head. Gently. Skinner's hand is big. It covers the whole top of the boy's head, like a cap. Protecting.

Secrets

The first thing you have to know is that Loretta is retarded. At least that's what my mother says. Long ago I looked "retarded" up in Webster's: "slow or limited in intellectual or emotional development" is the given definition. For what that's worth. Words. Words are a dime a dozen, my father says. He says there's something about a person who talks too much he doesn't much like.

Whenever he says that, I keep quiet. I have always been good at keeping quiet.

One thing you can say for Loretta is that she hardly talks at all. She never has. The first day of kindergarten I opened the coat closet door, and there she was, quiet as a mouse, rolled up on the closet floor. Her hair was black, her face was white, and her pink party dress speckled with chalk and lint. She was so small and quiet that at first I thought she was a doll. I thought the lint was stuffing leaking out. And then she spoke. "Josephine," she said in her wispy cotton-candy voice, and I was seized by terror. "Miss Jane!" I cried. Loretta grabbed my leg and held on tight. "Josephine," she said again, and in her eyes I saw a terror greater than my own. What could I do? "Okay," I said, and Loretta smiled, eyes bright as moonlight in the dusty closet.

Now how she even knew my name, when to my knowledge we had never met, was a mystery I did not pause to ponder. Even now the mystery remains. Reincarnation is a possible explanation. Who knows? I don't. What I do know is that for ten years there has been a mysterious bond between us, a bond about to be broken. Forever.

"Peculiar," is the word my mother uses to describe our association.

She has always refused to call it friendship, as if unable to believe that any normal human being could be friends with someone like Loretta.

Loretta, you see, has always been different. Very different. For one thing she has no parents. Imagine that! Instead of parents she has Jincey, who my mother says reminds her of a cleaning lady we once had. Mrs. Babson drank milky tea and wore black buckle boots in winter, boy's boots, the kind I always wanted. I liked Mrs. Babson; my mother didn't. She talked too much, my mother said, and smelled of mothballs. She didn't; she smelled of milky tea and lemon drops. But I kept quiet.

Jincey tells me that Loretta's mother died when Loretta was born, and I have sometimes wondered if it wasn't the fact of Loretta's retardation that did her in. After all, what a burden for a mother, a real mother, to bear. As for Loretta's father, he hired Jincey and then took off, though he does send money, and as Jincey says, "We want for nothing." It's true; they don't, and I have often thought how lucky for Loretta that it was Jincey who came along because Jincey loves Loretta, different as she is.

Now, I myself know what it is to feel different because for the first five years of my life I was an only child. It's a story my mother likes to tell of how when I was born the doctor patted her shoulder, and said I would be the one and only, and that she should go home and try and enjoy me. "Did he really say 'try'?" I asked her once.

"You were a good baby," said my mother. "Very good. You never cried at all."

Peter my brother, the sibling I had yearned for, cried all the time. "Colic," said the nurse. "Poor little boy," my mother said. Back and forth she walked in her sunny bedroom, winter light shining on her yellow hair. "Poor poor boy," she said. I was five years old with dark hair like my father's and a quiet face. Over my mother's shoulder I saw Peter's screaming mouth. Now he's nine with hair like sunlight; then he was bald. "Let me," I said, wanting to help. "Don't touch," said my mother, so I sat watching, wondering what would happen if I poked my finger hard into the soft spot on his head.

It is another of Loretta's differences that she was, and has remained, an only child. Naturally. Her mother is dead. Everyone in our class has lots of siblings. And everyone in our class, except for Loretta, is going away to boarding school. Next week!

It is the last and the largest of the differences that Loretta, unlike the rest of us, will never grow up. When I think about that I could weep. Weep! My only hope is that, to use my mother's word, she is too "retarded" to realize that she's being left behind.

For ten years now we have sat side by side, grade after grade at the Elm Tree School. The school is private, and so small that one great elm shades the building in spring and fall. The branches drift against each window. When I was little I used to think that private schools were those that were protected by trees, remember thinking too that when the windows rattled in winter, it was the elm tree whipping up the wind.

The mind of a child! It pleases me that I am practically grown up. "Time to put away childish things" as it says in the Bible. Juliet was married at fourteen. At fourteen I am going away to boarding school. Naturally I'm very excited.

When I visited last spring I thought it very pretty. Very, with white houses and green playing fields and blooming lilacs. The only thing that troubles me, a small thing really, is that being a girls' school they play softball. I don't mean to brag but baseball is one of my better sports. My best in fact. My father smiles when he sees me throw, and shakes his head. "You missed your calling, Josephine," he says.

I don't know about that, but what I'm going to miss is hardball. And, oh, how Loretta will miss me!

Because I am going away, so far away that I won't be back until Christmas, Hilda has been cooking all my favorite food. Last night, for instance, we had artichokes. I adore artichokes though my mother does not. Being a fastidious person she does not like what she calls "finger food." She is always careful about what she touches. Artichokes, she says, are barbaric, though not as barbaric as corn on the cob, because artichokes, at least, are quiet to eat.

Very quiet. Like secrets, I thought last night as slowly I plucked leaves, dipped them one by one in hollandaise, and pulled them through my teeth. Artichokes. I love the taste, love the way they last forever, the leaves growing pale and thin until at last the tastiest secret is revealed. The heart! The way it's hidden inside those prickles you'd never know that it was there.

Loretta, now, has never even tasted artichokes. Artichokes are a complicated vegetable, Jincey says, too complicated for someone like Loretta.

Most things, when you come right down to it, are too complicated for Loretta. "Remember," Jincey says, "her mind is the mind of a five-year-old." It makes me weep! At five I'd never even seen an artichoke, let alone tasted one. At five I didn't understand the meaning of the word. There was so much, at five, I didn't understand. At all.

For instance, Peter. One minute he wasn't there, the next he was. Folded in my mother's arms, he looked like a doll. Because she was holding him, I even thought he was, until he cried. "A son," my mother said, and I looked out the window where the sun shone red through falling leaves. "Your brother," said my mother, and then I knew. "His name is Peter."

Now that surprised me. Remember that at five my knowledge of the world was limited, and the only Peter I had ever known was Slovenly Peter, not a nice person at all with dirty hair and nails twenty inches long. Of course he was only a character in a book, my first book in fact, but at five it's sometimes difficult to tell the difference between fact and fiction. Which is the main reason I'm glad to be almost grown, and why just thinking of Loretta makes me weep. To live in a world where Slovenly Peter crouches in your closet and the Great, Red-Legged Scissor Man lies in wait beneath your bed can be a terrifying experience.

"Can I hold him?" I asked, mostly to be polite, because, frankly, he wasn't much to look at with his red face and wrinkled fingers.

"If you wear this," said my mother, holding up a small white mask. I was surprised, and somewhat bewildered. Did she think that I had germs? But I kept quiet; even then I was good at that. I shook my head, and sitting in the visitor's chair, I crossed my legs. "Where did he come from?" I asked my mother, making grown-up conversation.

How could I have known what I was asking? My mother's face turned red, and I thought, foolishly, that she was angry. I know better now. My mother is beautiful. My friends are always telling me, but they don't have to. I've always known. Her skin is smooth as glass, her eyes, like ice. As delicate, as fragile, as a snowflake. Even my father, when he lays his hand on her shoulder, does it carefully, as if afraid that she might break.

It's not easy for anyone to explain the facts of life to a five-year-old, certainly not a person as fastidious as my mother. She did her best, but what do words like "reproduction," "sperm," and "semen" mean to a young child? Nothing. Nothing at all. Words. They floated from her mouth and over my head, and in the end all I was able to catch and hold was "plant a seed."

Well, that at least made sense to me. Even at five I knew that if you planted a seed some kind of plant would grow. So all I needed was the right kind of seed, but what that was I didn't know, until the day the nurse was off and my mother took over.

That day I stood by and watched my mother changing Peter's diapers. I couldn't believe what I was seeing. "There's an ACORN in his crack!" I said, and at that very moment the acorn sprung a leak, squirting right up into my mother's face. And my mother laughed! Can you imagine my mother, always so careful about what touches her, laughing because somebody pees in her face?

That very night I lay in bed and tried to pee into the air. It didn't work. I soaked the sheet and my nightie, and my mother spanked me in the morning. She shook her head. "Shame," she said. "A big girl like you."

However, to make a long story short, once I knew that acorns were the answer, I gathered up fistfuls and planted them all. Now, of course, I have to wonder why. If one brother was a thorn in my side, what did I want with fifty more?

As I've said before, the mind of a child! I remember waiting for Peter's eyes to fall out because he cried so much. That's what happened in *Slovenly Peter;* there was even a picture of the girl with dark and empty sockets, her eyeballs staring from the ground. I was very careful never to cry, and my mother only had to read me the story of Little Suck-a-Thumb and the Great, Red-Legged Scissor Man once, and I stopped sucking my thumb. Forever. There in the picture was the boy's thumb caught between the blades, and in the last picture, he stood, looking sad, with both thumbs gone. I couldn't stop staring at that picture. I just couldn't.

Looking back, I suspect that was my mother's intention. "Take that dirty thing out of your mouth," she used to say, and I remember it was the "dirty" that surprised me. There is nothing cleaner-looking than a sucked thumb, pale and wrinkly, like a worm. "You look ridiculous," she said.

Peter never did suck his thumb. My mother made sure of that by giving him a pacifier from the start. If you want my opinion, a pacifier looks as ridiculous as a thumb. Maybe more. But I kept quiet.

Loretta now, she still sucks her thumb, and she's my age! Almost fifteen! Can you imagine! She still sits in Jincey's lap, too, which looks even more ridiculous, and it is all I can do not to laugh. I don't, of course, because it goes against the grain to hurt Loretta's feelings. Not that I haven't from time to time, especially when I was too young to know.

For instance, the first time I went to play, when I was five, Jincey, who sat nearby, "taking a load off" as she likes to say, suddenly held out her arms. To me! I was just so surprised. Already I felt too old for that sort of thing; in fact I couldn't even remember when last I'd sat in someone's lap. However, I didn't want to hurt her feelings, so slowly I inched across the room. My, but her lap was soft. She smelled like butter cookies, like Mrs. Babson's milky tea. She wrapped her arms around me and I settled back, just beginning to relax, when Loretta decided she wanted to sit there too. Well, that was that! There wasn't room for two of us, and as the strongest and the smartest, I was the one to go. "Retard," I hissed in Loretta's ear, not knowing what it meant, but knowing from the way I heard my mother say it that it was bad. And Loretta must have known that too. Because her eyes filled up with tears.

And I felt terrible. Just terrible. Because even at the age of five, I knew how much Loretta needed me.

"Polluted," my mother said when Loretta asked me to the beach. But she was not talking about Lake Michigan. The beach, you see, is public. It always has been, and always, when Loretta asks me, I go along. My mother, to give her credit, has never said no. Instead she shrugs. "I don't understand you, Josephine," she says.

Loretta loves the beach; I'm not sure why. She has never learned to swim. Over the years I've tried to teach her, but all she does is lie in the shallows, kicking her feet against wet pebbles, patting the sand with pudgy fingers. "Swimming, Josephine," she says, and smiles. Swimming! Poor Loretta. It breaks my heart.

Sunday we went to the beach for the last time. At least I knew it was the last time, but Loretta didn't. I haven't told her yet. Jincey sat on the sand under her orange beach umbrella, and Loretta and I sat on the jetty, kicking the water with our feet. I was kicking anyway; Loretta couldn't reach. The water flew from my toes in bright blue spangles, and Loretta, leaning against my shoulder, laughed. "Swimming!" she said.

Poor poor Loretta. How little she knows! How little she can do. Except, of course, to draw, and that, Jincey said, she was born knowing. Even in kindergarten no one could draw the way Loretta could.

She never did learn to read and write, but oh, how she could draw, and every year she did it better. At least *I* thought so. But not Miss Smith. Miss Smith, the art teacher, didn't like Loretta. People usually don't like what they don't understand.

There was one term, for instance, when the rest of us were working with clay, but not Loretta. Loretta did nothing but draw weeping willows, day after day. We stood pounding at our lumpy clay while Loretta sat, in her pink party dress and Mary Janes, scrunched over her paper. Beneath the pounding, we heard the waxy sweep of crayon. "What may I ask is that?" said Miss Smith, pointing a long red nail at the paper. Miss Smith wore her hair tight in a bun, and liked trees to look like trees.

I knew Loretta wouldn't answer, so I moved up next to her and looked Miss Smith right in the eye. "A weeping willow," I said. "Weeping." Miss Smith folded her arms across her bony chest and said, "I see." But I knew she didn't.

Because you don't *see* Loretta's drawings; you *feel* them. "She draws from the heart," says Jincey, and it's true. Loretta doesn't have a mind to get in the way, and in that soft and trailing green, you couldn't see the trees, but you could feel the sadness. Weeping, weeping. Jincey thinks Loretta may be famous one day. I think she may be right. Who knows? Stranger things have happened.

Like last Sunday at the beach when, sitting beside me on the jetty, Loretta suddenly began to sing. In ten years I had never heard her sing. There were no words, only her voice floating, sweet and high, over the blue water like a cloud. For some reason it sounded like a lullaby; for some reason it made me want to cry. So instead I dove off the jetty into the waiting water, and when I surfaced, Loretta clapped her hands. "Swimming, Josephine!" she said, sounding so proud I almost wept.

For some time now Jincey has been saying I should tell Loretta that I'm going away. A kindness, she says, to tell her now, give her some time to get used to it. "Probably she won't even understand," I said to Jincey. "You know better," Jincey said. But I don't. Not really.

Anyway, today I decided to give it a try, so I hopped on my bike and rode across town. Bending low over the handlebars, I watched the silver flicker of the spokes while overhead the oaks locked branches, and in my mouth the sweet and secret taste of last night's artichoke, lingering like a dream.

My town, I thought. A secret too. Streets hidden by trees, and houses by walls, and people by houses, by faces cool and smooth as glass.

I rode fast, along the lake, then curving inland, beyond the cemetery where the trees end and the sky surprises.

Jincey opened the door. "Why, our favorite visitor!" she said, just as she always does, which breaks my heart because I am their *only* visitor, but I kept quiet. She hugged me with her spicy-smelling hands. "How you've grown!" she said. Her head reached to my chin. Quickly, with one finger I touched her hair, felt the softness, saw silver threading brown. "Maybe it's you," I said. "Maybe you're shrinking," closing my eyes against the thought, seeing Jincey a small bright speck on the horizon, seeing her gone. Jincey laughed, a throaty sound like marbles in a chamois bag. "It happens," she said.

Loretta danced around us. "Lemon squares, lemon squares," she sang, and I could smell the lemony smell that matched the yellow walls. She took my hand and pulled me to the kitchen, where we sat at the round table and ate lemon squares and drank lemonade, and talked. At least I talked.

Which, when you come to think of it, is strange. It is the only place I do. It has always been that way: Jincey listens and Loretta draws, and I talk and talk.

"Smelting," Loretta said yesterday, patting my arm, patting her fresh white piece of paper. "Tell smelting now!"

"Loretta, you've heard that a hundred times already," I said, popping another lemon square in my mouth, licking the sugar from my fingers.

"Go on now," said Jincey. "It's your very best story, and besides, you'll be leaving us something to remember you by."

We looked at each other, Jincey and I, and I knew what she wanted, but I couldn't. Not yet.

"So, okay," I said. "Smelting it is."

Loretta squealed, and puckering up, blew kisses toward me, and I laughed. That's the thing about Loretta; when she doesn't make me cry, she makes me laugh. She can do the silliest things because she doesn't care what people think. She doesn't know enough to care, which is something I've always kept in mind when telling stories. Her mind, unlike mine, operates on the five-year-old level, and so I make sure my stories do too. So she can understand them.

"Once upon a time," I said, taking a deep breath, "long long ago and far away, when I was all of five years old, my father woke me on a dark October night. 'Get up,' he said. 'We're going smelting.' And I was scared. I didn't know what smelting was, and all around was wind and trees."

I heard Loretta's crayon hit the paper, making wind and blowing trees, and pulled my knees up to my chest to hug them.

"Five years old and frightened half to death. I would have sucked my thumb, but underneath my bed, the Great, Red-Legged Scissor Man was waiting. I lay in bed, my father leaning over me, and we were all alone. My mother gone without a word. To have a baby is what they said, but what that meant I didn't know.

"My father helped me dress. Clumsy and big, he pulled and

pinched, his strong weight bending, his breath a tickle on my cheek. 'There,' he said, and with a pail and a net and a silver light we went out, into the dark. And I was scared.

"He held my hand, and pointed the flashlight at the sky. 'Look,' he said. 'The moon.' I looked, but all I saw were big clouds skating, and branches clawing at the night. Under the moving trees we walked an acorn path.

"And then the trees were gone, and the clouds were gone, and we stood on the edge of the lake beneath the moon. The lake was a field of shining foil, alive and quiet as we walked down the path, across the beach, and out onto the jetty. 'When I was your age,' my father said, 'Dad took me smelting. It's your turn now.' And I was proud, not knowing why.

"I held the light, and my father dropped the net into the sleeping water, and then we waited. Waited and waited, I didn't know for what, and in the quiet I heard water breathing. Until it happened. 'Now!' said my father."

Loretta's crayon danced across the clouds and trees and sleeping water, jiggling in blue and silver waves.

"The water woke up, and where my light was shining, I saw silver dancing, and thought the world had tipped and stars were falling. 'They're coming,' said my father, and they came. THE SMELT. Hundreds, millions, they saw my light and they came swimming.

"And then my father lifted the net toward the light, the net alive with singing smelt. 'Good job,' my father said. We carried them home, and we cut off their heads, and fried them in oil, and ate them for breakfast, their tails too. All by ourselves."

I looked at Loretta, I looked at Jincey. "And that's the end," I said. I saw the sadness in her eyes and looked away. "You've never told it better," Jincey said, "that I remember."

Remember. At the door she put her arms around me, and for a moment I leaned against her, like a tree. A weeping willow. "Everything's going to be all right," she said. "No need to worry."

"Who's worrying?" I said. "Not me."

Loretta placed her picture in my hands. "Smelting!" she said. The sky and lake were soft as velvet, and smelt leapt, dancing, falling like tears down black black Night. I put the picture in my pocket. I looked at Jincey. "Tomorrow," I said.

Riding home, I slid beneath the trees and into darkness. The air was cold, and smelled of fall. Dusty leaves, dry roadside grass. Through dark leaves I saw flickers of pale sky. Like broken glass, I thought. I shivered.

The lake lay soft. I heard the juicy sound.

The wind was stinging. I opened my mouth to let the cold slide down inside. Leaning low, I rode fast, swinging my shoulders into turns, left and right, and left again, through the arched gate, down the graveled drive. And I was home.

"Look at you," my mother said.

She didn't look, but sat, her head bent, thrusting a silver needle up through the stiff canvas of her needlepoint. So I looked at her instead, saw the smooth white curve of her bent neck, imagining how, if I touched it, the skin would feel like ivory.

"Your hair," said my mother.

"The wind," I said. Smoothing it down, I settled quiet in a chair.

"I suppose you were at Loretta's again."

The fire crackled.

"Loretta?" said my father. "Who, may I ask, is that?"

"The retard," Peter said. Lying on the floor, his hair reflecting fire-light, my brother laughed.

"Shame on you," my mother said. She laughed, leaning to stroke his light bright hair. "Shame."

I looked away, keeping quiet, knowing that nothing would ease the ache.

For dinner we had artichokes.

"Again!" said Peter. He made a face.

"Josephine won't be back until Christmas," said my mother. I watched her fingers pluck the leaves, one by one, the delicate dipping into sauce. I leaned toward her. "Can I have your heart tonight?"

"It's my turn," Peter said, ripping the leaves in clusters, stacking them, uneaten, on his plate.

"You don't deserve it," I said.

"We'll see," said my mother.

"A toast," said my father. He raised his glass, winking as if we shared some secret. I winked back. "To boarding school!" he said. My mother smiled, and my throat ached.

"Some people have never even tasted artichoke," I said.

But no one heard.

Last night I dreamt that it was Christmas. I was home again, and nothing changed. Nothing. We sat together at the polished table. "One big happy family," said my father, his face creased by candlelight, and Peter, giggling, squirted milk through his teeth all over the table. My mother laughed. "Your presents," she said to me, pointing, and I was so excited. Boxes piled to the ceiling, and all for me! Box after box, and in each one an artichoke. Uncooked! "But I can't eat these," I said, trying to hide my disappointment. My mother shrugged, and I could tell she didn't care.

I woke up feeling awful, not knowing why, and then remembered that today I have to tell Loretta.

Why is it so hard to tell her? Why, I wonder, as I slowly dress. My trunk is packed. I walk around it to the door, liking it in daylight when the new black shines, liking the bright brass hinges, gold initials entwined like chains. But at night the dark shape weights the room, crouching in the corner like a coffin, I think.

I think as I walk down the stairs across the hall to the sun room where Hilda serves me eggs and bacon, toast and jam. My mother, from behind the paper, hears me chewing. "Anyone would think," she says, "you never got enough to eat." Anyone would think, I think, but I keep quiet. Tall and dark and thin, I am my father's child.

As a child, people would look me up and down. "A chip off the old block," they'd say to him, and I'd be proud, not knowing why.

How dark and full of mystery the world was then. How little I knew. How little Loretta knows, I think. Unfolding my legs, I ask to be excused. My mother nods. My bike waits gleaming in the cold garage, and I ride down shaded streets, thinking how to tell her so she'll understand, so the pain of my departure won't be so great. Fallen acorns scatter in my path, and swerving I avoid them. From little acorns big trees grow, I think, growing as I ride along the lake where light breaks free from trees to scatter across bright blue water. And then I know.

"How about a story," I say, crouching beside Loretta, who sits on the blue rug in the living room, a rainbow of crayons in her lap. She claps her hands, blows puckered kisses off her fingers. "Smelting?" she asks. I shake my head. "Better than that," I say. "A new and secret story just for you."

From the kitchen I smell sweet things baking, hear the soft rustle of waxed paper as Jincey packs a box of lemon squares for me to take away. "A very important story," I say, "so listen hard." Loretta shivers with excitement, and clutching her crayon, waits, poised above the clean white paper. I close my eyes.

"Once upon a time," I say, "long long ago, when I was five years old and Peter just a baby, my father was outside raking leaves, and I was outside watching.

"The sun was hot, the air was cold. It was fall, and everything was falling, leaves and acorns, smelts and stars. Inside the house my mother walked from room to room with Peter crying in her arms. Even through the windows I heard the crying, heard my mother crooning, poor little boy, poor poor boy. Their cheeks were touching.

"'You're in the way,' my father said.

"The leaf pile grew, spreading across my sneakers, up to my knees. Dusty leaves, all dry and dead. I stepped back, hugging myself in the cold air, the sun hot on my head, and was waiting. Waiting, and waiting, I wasn't sure for what. And then my father looked at me.

"And it was then I knew.

"'Close your eyes,' my father said. He dropped his rake and turned away. But though I held my breath, I didn't close my eyes because, remember, I was only five, and frightened of the dark.

"'Taking a leak,' I'd heard my father say before, but it was like a waterfall, a rainbow in the sun, curving up and out and down. As for the acorn, why, it had grown into a tree! Watching, I held my breath, hardly able to believe my eyes. And though I've always been good at keeping quiet, this time I couldn't.

"'I wish,' I said to my father when he was back to raking again. 'I wish I could do that.'

"'Do what?' my father said, leaves rustling underneath his rake.

"'You know,' I said, 'What you do.'

"He looked at me. 'You can,' he said.

"'When?' I asked, not daring to believe, and leaning on his rake, he smiled.

"'When you're big,' he said. 'When you're big. Like me.'"

"And that's the story."

In the silence I hear Loretta's crayon move against the paper. My eyes still closed, I hug my knees.

"All done," she says, placing her picture on my lap. "All done." She sounds so pleased.

"What's this!" I say, unable to believe my eyes.

Against blue sky leaves drift and swirl like drops of blood, the green grass littered, stained with red. Against one pile two yellow rakes are leaning, one large, one small. Not touching. Sad.

"Loretta," I say, speaking slowly. "He was *not* talking about raking leaves! Weren't you even listening?"

Loretta touches my wrist. "Smelting now?" she asks. Her fingers are soft. I pull away.

"Smelting happened once, Loretta. Once! It's dead, finito!"

"I know," Loretta says. "I know."

"You don't," I say. "You don't know anything!"

She leans toward me, her round eyes bright with unshed tears. If I shook her, her eyes would empty, tears rolling down.

"Listen now, and listen hard!" I say. "I'm leaving you. I'm going away, to boarding school."

I see her eyes widen. I see her struggling to understand. But what is boarding school to someone like Loretta? Words. Nothing more.

"Raking!" I say, disgusted. "Who wants to rake leaves? Where's the future in that?"

But what does "future" mean to someone like Loretta? Nothing. Naturally. She is too retarded to comprehend.

"Listen," I say. "You are about to lose your one and only friend. That means no more visiting, no more hugging, no more talking."

"No more smelting?"

"You got it."

In her eyes I see the slow surprise, the understanding shining through. I think of artichokes, the slow unpeeling, revealing of the secret hidden heart as reaching up, she wraps her arms around my neck and rubs her cheek against my own.

"Poor Josephine," she croons.

"Not *me*," I say, trying to pull away.

Loretta holds on tight. "Poor Josephine. Poor poor girl."

"No," I whisper. "You don't know what you're talking about."

"I love you, Josephine," Loretta says.

Words. Words are a dime a dozen, and what can poor Loretta know of love? I feel an aching in my heart as Loretta folds me in her pale arms, and rocks me back and forth. "I love you, Josephine," she says, and rocking, I feel my heart expand, burst like a flower into bloom.

Pandora

In the spring Hugo always woke early. The sun was just rising, light filling the room slowly like water poured into crystal. Beside him, Rosamund slept soundly, curled on her side. She never woke before six-thirty, and from the quality of the light, Hugo knew it was closer to five. He lay still, listening to the mournful cooing of the doves. When he heard the hall clock strike, he pushed back the covers, and tightening his stomach, began to pound his fists against it.

"Must you?" Rosamund murmured.

"I heard the clock." Because of the pounding, the words exploded in short gasps. Rosamund sat up.

"Hugo! It's five-thirty, not six-thirty!"

"Sorry," he said, not sorry at all. Sitting up, he kissed her cheek. "Do you feel different?"

She looked past him, out the window. "What?" she said.

"Our birthday," he said, kissing her again. Her cheek felt warm and slightly fuzzy, like the skin of a peach. "Can you believe we're forty?"

"Easily," she said, smiling, briefly, as she swung out of bed. "We were thirty-nine yesterday."

Hugo watched her disappear into the bathroom. The mattress, without their balanced weight, sagged in the middle. An expensive mattress, and they had taken such care, turning it once a month for the last eighteen years. Hugo had assumed it would last a lifetime. He sighed, and rising too, followed her into the bathroom.

"What time is Jeremy coming?" he asked.

"Ten-thirty-five. That's when his plane gets in."

Hugo watched in the mirror as she pulled her nightgown over her head. As she bent to spread the bathmat, her dark hair fell across her breasts. She bent easily, dipping and rising in one fluid motion. She didn't know Hugo was watching. "Imagine coming all the way from England for a birthday party," he said.

"But he always does!" She looked at him, saw his eyes in the mirror. Her eyes went dark. "It wouldn't be a party without him." Turning away, she stepped into the shower.

"Absolutely," Hugo said. "You're right." He brushed and flossed and shaved. The sun rose above the cedars. The mirror sparkled. He smelled soap and toothpaste, yellow lilies and new-cut grass. "But we've been so lucky, Rosamund. Do you suppose he envies us?"

He could see the outline of her body behind the curtain. Head back, arms up, she was washing her hair. He heard the splash of water running. "Hugo, he's our oldest friend!" She turned off the water. "Could you hand me a towel?" Hugo handed her a towel.

After breakfast they went outside, Rosamund to cut flowers for the party, Hugo to fix a weak board in the front stoop. As he wrenched it loose, he felt something tweak in his back, not a pain exactly, but an unfastening. Straightening slowly, he waited. It felt all right.

The board, though, had come away too easily, the rot far worse than he'd imagined. Hugo looked up at the house. Over the years the house had settled, causing the eaves to dip in what Hugo had always thought of as a graceful curve. Now, suddenly, it frightened him. Now, for all he knew, termites were chewing their way through buried foundation walls.

"Hugo." Rosamund came across the lawn, her long legs making scissor shadows on the grass. "What are you doing?" Hugo looked at her, and shook his head.

"You haven't changed at all," he said. He smiled.

"Is that a compliment?"

"Of course." He looked across the lawn to the garden. The snow peas were already halfway up the trellis. "Rosamund," he said. "Do you think it was a mistake, not to have children?"

"But Hugo, we never wanted any! What's gotten into you today?"

"I don't know. The rot, I guess. I'm afraid the whole house might be riddled with it."

"Don't worry about what you can't see. Here." She handed him a sprig of lilacs. "Happy Birthday," she said. "Thank you," said Hugo. He held the lilacs gently. Lilacs, like gardenias, distressed him; they seemed to bruise so easily, die so quickly. "Come on," said Rosamund. "Let's do our presents, before Jeremy arrives."

They sat together on the terrace. Hugo opened his presents first, two bottles of their favorite wine and a set of barbells he had wanted. "No more exercising in bed," Rosamund said. Hugo laughed. He gave Rosamund two bottles of their favorite wine, the gardening cart she'd asked for, and the same small leather notebook he gave her every year. "What a gloomy color," Rosamund said, looking at the smooth black leather. "We've reached a certain age," Hugo said. "Can you believe we've been married nineteen years?" Rosamund opened the book, laying her hand flat on the clean white page. "Yes," she said. Hugo looked at her hand, at the slight puckering of skin around the knuckles. It was the nineteenth notebook he had given her. "Your secret books," he called them. "Not secret," she said, "boring." She had showed him a page once, an entry from one of their trips. She mentioned the weather, their meals, their purchases, and the sights they'd seen. "I wouldn't call it boring," he'd said, hedging. "A little dry, perhaps." Rosamund had smiled. "I told you," she said. She kept them squirreled away; Hugo had no idea where.

"If you don't need me," he said, "I guess I'll cut the lawn."

"I don't need you." Carefully she folded the wrapping paper, smoothing out the creases. "I wonder what Jeremy's bringing us," she said. "He sounded so excited on the phone."

"He always does."

"He gives the most wonderful presents."

"Because he knows us so well," Hugo said, rising.

"Exactly," said Rosamund. "He never has to ask us what we need."

The grass didn't need cutting, but Hugo felt like pushing. The heavy mower slid over the cropped lawn like a hand over velvet. Hugo moved back and forth, back and forth, until he felt sweat trickling down his neck. But the lack of resistance beneath the blades bored him; there was nothing to strain against. He imagined using a scythe, the satisfaction there must be in that long smooth sweep of the arm, the ache of hard-worked muscles tightening. But what was the point in imagining that when he cut the grass weekly from April through September.

Breaking away, Hugo began to move erratically across the lawn. Using the grass as paper, the mower as pen, he wrote his name and Rosamund's and enclosed them in a heart. He cut an arrow through the center. He was glad Rosamund was in the kitchen, where she couldn't see him. He had no idea why he was doing this.

Starting on the outer edge, Hugo began to circle the lawn, moving slowly toward the center. "Things fall apart, the center cannot hold." Yeats. He hadn't thought of Yeats in years. Once, long ago on the banks of the Severn, he had recited "The Second Coming" to Rosamund. It was his favorite poem. She sat beside him, listening, watching the swans glide past. When he was done, he waited. Rosamund closed her eyes. They had been married six months. "Are you always so dreary?" she said. She said it gently, the words softened by a smile.

Rosamund. His touchstone. Over the years they had grown together like two bushes planted side by side.

"A still life," Jeremy had said just last year as he looked at them standing together in the newly painted kitchen. The white walls and gleaming floor held the sunlight like champagne. "Is that a compliment?" said Rosamund, and Jeremy had laughed. "But of course!" he said.

Jeremy had a peculiar laugh, a series of small round sounds that bubbled up from somewhere deep inside. He laughed a great deal, often, it seemed to Hugo, for no apparent reason. "Jeremy," Hugo had said that night at dinner, "don't you think it's time you found a job?"

"What a hideous notion!" Jeremy said, laughing again. "Can you see me stuck behind a desk reading bad novels?"

"Not that," said Hugo, who was trade book editor at Bradford and Brown. "Something that suits you. Theater or film."

"But there's no need!"

"We have money too, you know."

"Hugo," Rosamund said. "You're being a prig."

Slowly the circles tightened. By the time Hugo reached the center, he was drenched in sweat. He supposed he was a bit of a prig. Perhaps he was envious. Jeremy, too, was almost forty, but there was an ageless-ness about him, an elusive quality that Hugo found both irritating and endearing. When he wasn't with them, Hugo had difficulty remember-ing his face.

He stood motionless on the lawn. The sun, coming through the tight new leaves, dappled the grass, the long steep roof. Nothing moved. Hugo stared at the house, soothed by its loveliness. He was ashamed of the passion he felt for the house; he mentioned it to no one, not even Rosamund.

Pushing out from the center, Hugo began to retrace his steps. He liked moving out in widening circles, liked the slow unwinding, spiral-ing toward the outer edge. He thought of the shells Jeremy had once brought Rosamund, beautiful shells, some fragile as porcelain. Rosa-mund, afraid the shells might break, kept them in a glass case, lying flat so that only the spirals showed. When Rosamund was out, Hugo liked to hold them. Cupping a conch in his palm, he would thrust his finger into the cool dark center. So cool and smooth it felt damp, as if the sea's moisture were trapped inside.

Rosamund was right; Jeremy did give good presents. Like Jeremy himself, they were always unexpected, always a surprise. Walking faster now, Hugo pushed the mower toward the garage, wondering what it could be that Jeremy was bringing them this time.

"You'll never guess," Jeremy said, setting the wicker basket down on the kitchen table. Lifting the lid, he reached inside. "Her name," he said, holding the small white puppy like an offering, "is Pandora!"

Rosamund stared at the dog, Hugo at Jeremy. Jeremy had pale eye-brows that sprang upward at the ends like angel wings, so pale that Hugo seldom noticed them. Now, against the pallor of his face they looked dark. His face seemed thinner, and there were shadows beneath his eyes. "Was it a bad flight?" Hugo asked.

Jeremy set the puppy on the table. "A Samoyed," he said, stroking the soft fur. "From Siberia. Thorpe had a litter. I couldn't resist." He laughed.

"Who's Thorpe?" said Hugo.

"I don't believe it, Jeremy. You know we don't like dogs!" Rosamund's face was pinched and tight. Hugo had never seen her quite so angry.

"We don't really know, Rosamund," Hugo said, embarrassed by her rudeness. "We've never owned one."

"Because we've never wanted one!" She left the room.

"I'm sorry," Hugo said.

"Not to worry," said Jeremy. He ran his finger along the curve of the dog's mouth. "Look," he said, "she knows how to smile."

"She's very sweet," said Hugo, "but are you sure you wouldn't like to keep her for yourself?"

"Heavens, no! I bought her for you. A token of my affection. Remembrance of things past."

"What are you talking about? Are you going away?"

Jeremy laid his hand on Hugo's shoulder. His fingers felt cool. Comforting. Hugo had always admired Jeremy's physical ease. In the market he would touch a stranger on the wrist. "I do like your shirt!" he'd say, and the stranger would smile, both pleased and startled.

Jeremy slid his arm across Hugo's back. "I'm always going away."

"But are you sure you feel all right?"

"Can one call boredom a disease?"

"Boredom?"

Jeremy laughed. "What amazes me, Hugo, is that in all these years you haven't changed at all." He yawned. "I could do with some sleep," he said. "The flight seemed long. And Hugo," Jeremy stood in the doorway, "if I don't get a chance to talk to Rosamund, will you tell her?"

"Tell her what?" said Hugo. But Jeremy had already gone upstairs.

"Rosamund," Hugo said that night as they lay in bed, "I think you hurt his feelings."

"He hurt mine."

Hugo looked at her. In the moonlight she was the color of marble. Through the floorboards he heard the whimpering of the puppy, the muted roar of the dishwasher. The party had been a great success.

"I don't think he looked very well," Hugo said. He waited. "I thought he looked sick, Rosamund. Very sick, as if. . . ."

"You're so morbid." She rolled over, facing the wall. "I wish you'd stop it."

"We don't have to keep her," Hugo said. Rosamund said nothing. Hugo put his hand on her bare shoulder. Cold and still, it felt like stone. He tucked both hands beneath the covers. "Don't worry," he said. "We can tell him in the morning."

But in the morning, Jeremy was gone. "Not even a note," said Hugo. "I don't understand."

Rosamund stood in front of the bureau, her hands flat, pressing down, as if testing its weight.

"I do," she said. Her voice was dead.

Hugo saw her face in the mirror above the bureau. He saw that her eyes were dark as night. She stared, unblinking, into them. "It's over," she said. Did she think Jeremy was dying too? He didn't dare ask.

He turned away, looking out across the lawn he'd mowed the day before. Nothing showed. Sunlight lay in quiet pools on short green grass. Overhead the elm spread graceful branches; on one he saw an oriole's nest, half hidden by leaves. As he watched, an oriole shot like a flash of fire through the green. Hugo saw a strand of tinsel in its beak. He swallowed to ease the tightness in his throat.

"At least we'll have the dog," he said.

"We will not!" said Rosamund. "In case you've forgotten, we both work. Dogs need time and attention." She turned to Hugo. "They need love."

Hugo watched as the oriole wove the tinsel into the nest. The nest swayed, shimmering. He guessed the tinsel came from last year's Christmas tree. He imagined a nest woven from the puppy's fur, the pure white gleaming against green and gold.

"We'll find somebody who wants her," Rosamund said.

Hugo turned. The bed was between them. "I do," he said.

The summer was the most beautiful in years, warm blue days and cool clear nights. As always Hugo and Rosamund took August off, but this year, instead of traveling, they stayed home.

Hugo was glad. Never had he felt such abundance of time. He pruned wisteria and replaced the stoop. He painted the shutters, stacking them like giant dominoes on the lawn. As he painted, Pandora slept beside him on the grass, her fur like milkweed against his skin. Wherever he went, Pandora followed.

Rosamund worked the garden, moving carefully down the rows. Hugo watched her bend with slow deliberation toward the flowers. These days it seemed she seldom looked his way. He worried she might be jealous of the dog.

"I'll give her away if she's any trouble," said Hugo, embarrassed by the pleading in his voice.

He heard her scissors cut and clip.

"Why are you angry? Don't be angry."

She closed her eyes. "I'm not angry."

"What then?" But she didn't answer. He hated to have her so upset. "She's sweet, Rosamund," said Hugo. "Jeremy thought so too."

"What does he know," Rosamund said.

Jeremy called from Oxford on the seventeenth. The connection was terrible, crackling with static. A moment of silence followed each word; it was like speaking into a void. "Why did you leave like that?" Hugo asked. He imagined the words flying through thick black cables on the ocean floor, springing like birds into the misty Oxford air. "We love her," Hugo shouted. He held the phone to Rosamund who shook her head. "We're worried," he said. "How are you?" There was a bubbling sound, whether laughter or static Hugo couldn't tell. The line went dead. "We were cut off," said Hugo.

"Would you mind keeping her away from me," Rosamund said, pointing to Pandora, who was rubbing against her leg.

"She only wants a pat," said Hugo.

"Keep her away!"

Hugo kept her away. He took Pandora for long walks, along the railroad tracks, and through the woods. There was no need for a leash; he had only to call and she would come. Hugo decided to try jogging again. He had tried it before, but the harsh sound of his breathing had frightened him. What if his heart should give out when he was alone? He had heard of it happening to others his age. Now with Pandora, he felt safe.

Every evening they went for a run along the tracks. The tracks were deserted, and, underfoot, the cinders soft as they ran east toward the ocean. In the setting sun, Pandora's fur was tipped with gold. Whenever he looked, her black eyes danced.

By the end of August they were doing two miles a day, and Hugo's stomach felt hard and firm.

On the first of September Pandora was six months old. In June Hugo had been able to cup her in his hands. A bowl of cream. Now she was too large for his lap, though she still tried, whenever he sat, to climb into it. What touched Hugo was the frenzy of her love. She liked to lean against him, thrusting her cool nose into his hand. When he talked to her, she listened, head cocked, her body tense with concentration.

"I never knew a dog could be such fun," Hugo said to Rosamund, who was canning tomatoes at the stove. He could hardly see her through the steam. Outside the window Pandora sat on the terrace, her tail waving like a feathered plume. The noon whistle blew, and Pandora, raising her head, howled like a wolf.

"That's the most terrible noise," said Rosamund.

"It's in the blood, you know." Hugo leaned toward her. "They're part wolf. The Eskimos use them to herd reindeer, and to sleep with the children too. A kind of blanket and bodyguard."

Rosamund counted the newly processed jars. "Fifteen more than last year," she said, adding the number to her list.

"Couldn't you try to like her?"

"I don't like dogs." Carefully she dried each jar and placed them on the sill to cool.

"I didn't either. Pandora's different."

Rosamund turned a page in her notebook. "Seventeen more than the year before."

"Besides, Rosamund, Jeremy gave her to us."

She looked at him. The sunlight, coming through the windows, turned the steam to gold, illuminated her face. "Have you ever wondered why?" she said. Hugo was surprised, not by how much the light revealed, but how little.

A postcard came, sent from Nepal. It was the kind of thing Jeremy was always doing. His magic trick, they called it, his tendency to disappear, resurfacing in the most unlikely place. He sent his love. He said the sky was the color of Rosamund's eyes. On the front of the card a monastery clung to a white-faced mountain.

"Remember," said Hugo, "he mentioned your eyes the day we met." Rosamund was silent for so long that Hugo thought she hadn't heard. "I remember," she said at last.

They had been married for six months, at Oxford for three. A cloudless June day, and they walked toward the river, Hugo carrying an umbrella in case of rain. Jeremy appeared from nowhere. Tall and thin. Golden. "Marvelous!" He held out his arms. "You must be twins." His pale curls glistened in the sun. "Married," Hugo said, hoping to be rid of him, but Rosamund had smiled in her careful way. "We have the same birthday though. June twenty-first."

"Ah, Gemini! That explains it then." He looked at the sky, he looked at Rosamund. "Your eyes," he said, "are bluer." And, surprisingly, Rosamund had laughed. Though nothing amusing had been said, she tipped her head and laughed, a young laugh Hugo had never heard before. And Jeremy had smiled at both of them, his whole face, eyes, mouth, eyebrows, curving upward, smiling with such pleasure, such apparent delight, that Hugo had to smile too.

Hugo stared at the postcard in his hand. The monastery was perched so precariously on the cliff that it seemed held aloft by faith alone. He felt a sudden stab of longing for Jeremy. Jeremy, like the bright tinsel in the oriole's nest, was so woven into their lives that it was impossible to imagine life without him. "I hate to think of him alone."

"What makes you think he is," said Rosamund.

"What do you mean?" asked Hugo, but Rosamund didn't answer.

The nights grew crisp, the days short, and only asters were blooming in the garden. Pandora's coat thickened for winter, and she whimpered now when Hugo brushed her. Only the under layer was still soft, like feathers against his fingers. She had been with them for five months, and still Rosamund kept her distance.

"I wish," Hugo said, and stopped. There was nothing he could say. There had always been silence between them, a shared silence. A bond. Together they had created a life, exquisite, orderly, contained. "Why did you marry me?" Hugo had asked her once, and when, after a moment, she had said, "You made me safe," Hugo had understood. He felt the same.

Nothing had changed. Yet here he was, suddenly feeling that they, like the monastery, were held in place by fragile threads. Suddenly he felt the silence, not as a bond but barrier. It frightened him.

He pushed the fear away. He stroked Pandora's head, and looked at Rosamund across the table. The candles were lit, and the dim light created distance. He saw her as Jeremy must have seen her, lovely and mysterious, grave and charming.

"I never knew Americans could be so charming," Jeremy's mother had said with some surprise.

"Really, Mother!" Jeremy said, laughing. "You're impossible!"

She was, and so was Jeremy's father. They smelled of dogs, and had a way of peering at Jeremy as if they couldn't quite remember who he was. "Which is just as well," said Jeremy, "because when they do remember, they disapprove."

"Maybe you were adopted," Rosamund said.

Jeremy smiled at her; he smiled at Hugo. "I have been!" he said.

"He'll probably show up for Christmas," Hugo said to Rosamund.

Rosamund stared into the candle flame. "No," she said with such conviction that Hugo was surprised. How could she be so sure? She was still staring at the candle, and Hugo stared too, waiting for something to be revealed.

The journal he had given her lay on her desk. He opened it. His heart was pounding. In nineteen years he had never done such a thing. On the first page she'd written the date, their birthday, and one word, so heavily crossed out that Hugo couldn't read it. Nothing else. The rest was blank.

The first snow fell in November. Waking early, Hugo heard Pandora yapping in the kitchen. Now that it grew dark by five, they ran in the morning before Hugo left for work. Outside, the ground was covered, the air thick with falling snow. All the familiar landmarks had disappeared, and Hugo let Pandora lead. He was impressed by the agility with which she sidestepped rocks and other obstacles he couldn't see. She herself was scarcely visible except when she turned, and then he saw her dark eyes gleaming. Their feet made no sound; they might be flying. Hugo flung up his arms and whooped with joy.

"It was like running through a dream," he said to Rosamund at breakfast. His cheeks were flushed, his body tingled.

Rosamund looked at him over her coffee cup. "Really?" she said. Hugo was surprised by the pity he felt. "I wish you'd come with us." He wasn't surprised when she shook her head.

At night Hugo lay in bed. Rosamund slept beside him, curled like a shell. The blanket of snow intensified the silence. He thought of the blank white pages in Rosamund's journal. He thought of Jeremy lying in a bare stone cell on a white mountain. Alone. He pushed the thoughts away. He stretched his legs, feeling the ridge of muscles along his thighs. He had never been in better shape. Perhaps, in the spring, he'd try the marathon.

In January another card arrived, this time from Greece. "At least he's someplace warm," said Hugo. There was a photograph of a ruined temple, and on the back, printed in large block letters, the word CIAO.

Rosamund was whipping egg whites for an apricot souffle. Hugo sat at the table, inserting linen napkins into silver rings. "He didn't even send a present this year," said Rosamund. The whisk rapped sharply against the metal bowl. Hugo held a thin ring up to his eye. "I spy," he said, hoping to make her laugh. Instead he saw a tear slide slowly down her cheek. He had never seen her cry. He looked away. "Did you know that Pandora in Greek means 'having all gifts?'" he said.

The whites rose in snowy peaks above the bowl. "I know the myth," she said.

"Delicious!" Hugo said when the souffle was done. He hoped to please her, but Rosamund was staring at her plate. "I don't think I can bear it," she said, so quietly that she seemed to be talking to herself. Perhaps she was. "Delicious," Hugo said again.

In January the cold set in. People said there hadn't been such a winter in years. The ground was frozen four feet deep, and birds toppled from trees, falling like small lumps of coal. Pandora became increasingly restless, always whining to be let out. Though Rosamund seemed indifferent to the noise, Hugo found it irritating. "She thinks she's in Siberia," he said. He heard the rustle of pages turning. "What are you reading?"

"A book," said Rosamund.

Hugo pressed his forehead against the window. Outside was dark. He felt wind coming through the cracks. Whining, Pandora circled his legs. "What's happening?" he said. He heard the rustle of another page. "Nothing," said Rosamund.

"All right then, go out," he said to Pandora, opening the door. "No one's stopping you." He closed the door hard; the windows rattled.

Later he went to call her in. He stood in the cold, calling, imagining Pandora lying by the road, a drifting of snow. A full moon threw shadows across white lawn. "She's been killed," he said to Rosamund. "I know it." Rosamund closed her book. "You don't know anything," she said. And sure enough, soon after Hugo heard Pandora whining to come in.

The last day of the month a blizzard closed down schools and offices for three days. Pandora spent all her time outdoors, digging tunnels in the snow. Rosamund lay in bed, and Hugo sat by the fire, a pile of unread manuscripts on the table, and thought of warmth. He felt the cold this winter as he never had before, chilling him no matter how he dressed. He supposed it was his age. He stared into the flames and longed for summer, for hot dry days, long hot nights.

He remembered a summer Jeremy had taken them to Devon, to a small inn with a thatched roof, and a cock that crowed at dawn. Day after day of hazy heat, the three of them walking, arm in arm, down quiet lanes.

One day Hugo stopped to fish in a small dark stream, and Rosamund and Jeremy went on ahead, following the path onto the moor. The water was smooth as glass, flowing soundlessly beneath ancient oaks. After an hour with not even a strike, Hugo went to find them.

After the shadowed stream, the intensity of the light was almost blinding, the moor shimmering under a vast pearl-colored sky. High summer. Nothing moved, the only sound the hum of bees. Hugo called loudly, but his voice, swallowed by sky, was thin and small. He found them finally, sitting side by side on a flat-topped tor. Hugo did not like heights. Slowly he climbed the steep rock, moving cautiously to avoid the bees. Jeremy peered down, smiling. "You're not afraid, are you?"

"Of course not!" Hugo said in a loud and frightened voice. How Jeremy and Rosamund had laughed. Hugo hadn't really minded, though it always surprised him to hear Rosamund laugh. He had known when he married her that if she had a flaw it was her lack of humor. "Is that supposed to be funny?" she'd say when Hugo told a joke.

Hugo sighed. He couldn't remember when he'd last heard her laugh. He missed Jeremy. He wished that instead of Greece, Jeremy had chosen Spain or Italy. Greece, to Hugo, was where poets went to die.

Hugo went upstairs. Rosamund, still in her nightgown, had a book open in her lap. She did not appear to be reading. "Do you suppose that someone could actually die from boredom?" he said, not wanting to mention Jeremy by name. Rosamund looked past him, out the window.

"Yes," she said.

There was a short thaw and then the cold came back. Snow turned to ice that glittered like shards of broken glass. When Pandora tried to dig her tunnels, her paws skittered across the frozen crust. Lifting her head, she howled, her breath like smoke in brittle air.

Hugo raised the window. "Shut up!" he yelled. When Rosamund looked at him, he shrugged.

That night he lay in bed, listening to the creak of joists and beams adjusting to the cold. He imagined a sudden collapse, the old house caving in upon itself, he and Rosamund buried in debris. He wondered if they could survive such a fall, if anyone could. The cold was intense. Despite three blankets and a quilt, he shivered. Rolling on his side, he drew up his knees and hugged them to his chest. He could not stop shivering. Closing his eyes, he waited for sleep. He waited.

On February 14 a letter arrived, a thin blue envelope with an Oxfordshire postmark. Hugo held it out to Rosamund, who shook her head. He turned the envelope over. "It's from his parents." His hands were trembling. He opened it slowly. "What do you know!" he said. "He's married! He married Julia Thorpe."

"You sound surprised." Rosamund sat on the sofa, her head bent over a small embroidered pillow in her lap. Her face was hidden. She was completely motionless except for her fingers, plucking at the pillow.

"But I thought he was dying. I thought they were writing to say he was dead."

Hugo watched her fingers plucking, pulling at the fabric as if to rip

it. "He is," she said in a voice that came from somewhere else, an echo
in an empty shell.

"Don't," Hugo said. He sat beside her, and touched her wrist.
"You'll hurt it." Lifting her hand, he held it in his own. Her wrist was
limp. He squeezed it gently. "Everything's going to be fine," he said.
"We have each other." Rosamund said nothing. He squeezed her hand
again. "I love you," he said. He waited. He heard the clock ticking in
the hall. And again he squeezed her hand, this time hard enough so that
he heard her knuckles crack. She looked at him as if she'd forgotten he
was there. "Did you hear me?" he asked. Rosamund pulled her hand
away. "Yes," she said.

Late winter. A time of year he'd never liked. He still ran with Pandora in the morning, but the pleasure was gone. Though the snow had
melted, the ground was still frozen, ringing like iron beneath his feet.
The sky was heavy, the color of slate; its weight oppressed him.

Pandora began to shed her winter coat. Clumps of fur clung to rugs
and chairs. Hugo waited for Rosamund to complain, but to his surprise,
she never said a word. He combed Pandora nightly, filling bags with
coarse fur bristling with burrs and twigs. The steel comb pulled, and
Pandora whimpered when Hugo approached her, comb in hand. To
keep her down Hugo had to straddle her, rising only to heave her from
side to side.

One night as he was combing her, Pandora began to growl. Hugo
rapped her on the nose with the steel comb. The growling deepened.
"Bitch," said Hugo. "Who do you think you are?" He raised the comb
again.

"You're hurting her," said Rosamund.

"Look at her fur," said Hugo. "A Goddamn mess."

Rosamund sighed. "All right," she said. She knelt beside Pandora,
touching the dog's nose with her finger. Pandora licked it, whimpering,
then gently took her wrist.

Hugo looked at the dog's sharp teeth, at Rosamund's skin.

"She'll bite you."

Rosamund shook her head. "It makes her feel safe," she said.

The dog lay quiet on the floor between them. After a moment Hugo
began to comb. He combed carefully, using his fingers when he could.

From time to time Pandora whimpered, but that was all. She didn't move. Perhaps, thought Hugo, everything would be all right. He heard the ticking of the kitchen clock, heard water dripping from the eaves.

"It's time to plant the garden," Hugo said.

And Rosamund sighed. "Hugo," she said. "There's something I should tell you."

"No," said Hugo. He bent above Pandora, careful not to look at Rosamund's face.

"Hugo."

"No!" said Hugo, and Rosamund drew her hand away and stood.

"I think maybe you already know," said Rosamund.

Hugo did not stop combing. He combed hard and fast. Rosamund stood above him, her shadow falling across the fur.

"Get out of the way," said Hugo.

The shadow moved.

The comb caught fur. Pandora whimpered. Hugo pulled, and deep in her throat, Pandora growled.

"Bitch!" said Hugo.

Pandora tried to rise, but Hugo, straddling, pushed her down. The comb, still caught, lifted the dog's head from the ground. Hugo yanked. Pandora yelped, a single cry, and turning, sank her teeth into Hugo's arm.

The sudden pain took Hugo by surprise. Falling back, he let her go. Pandora scrambled to her feet and fled.

Hugo sat there, watching the slow welling of his blood. He shook his head.

"She bit me."

Rosamund stood, arms folded, in the doorway, standing as if poised for flight.

"Hugo," she said. "You knew she would."

Hugo licked his arm. He tasted blood. The pain diminished, transformed to a throbbing ache. But he said nothing. What was there left to say?

He was suddenly exhausted. He sat on the floor, his eyes closed, hearing nothing but the beating of his heart.

Civil War

Eliot Jarvis smelled Sue Ellen the minute she stepped through the door. He sniffed loudly. Orange blossoms and honey. "I'll take her," he said.

Louise sighed. If only she wasn't so tired. In the three weeks she'd been down she hadn't had one good night's sleep. All night, every night, a mockingbird sang outside her window. She dreamt of broken glass, woke to the slither of lizards on the roof. Her back ached from the soft mattress.

She was so tired that her father's behavior no longer embarrassed her.

"We think the stroke has affected more than his legs," she said quietly to Sue Ellen.

Sue Ellen walked over to the bed. "Hey, Mr. Jarvis," she said. "Are you crazy?" She tapped him lightly on the forehead.

Eliot opened his eyes. Because of his cataracts, he saw little more than shadow, but the scent of orange blossoms was stronger than before.

"Whose side are you on?" he said.

"Yours, I think," said Sue Ellen, "but I need to know what I'm letting myself in for."

Louise felt a headache coming on; she pressed her fingers to her forehead. Her knuckles cracked. "He's talking about the Civil War." she said.

"The South will rise again," said Eliot, lifting a trembling fist into the air.

Sue Ellen caught his wrist and lowered it gently to the sheets. Light as a feather, she thought. She thought of birds. A baby bird. She shivered.

"My father thinks the wrong side won." Louise closed her eyes. Oh, the pain in her head. She should never have let Sue Ellen in the door. Her hair was too long, her breasts too large. She wore red sandals and her toes looked dirty.

"Don't think," said Eliot. "I know."

"I like the South myself," Sue Ellen said. "The sun, you know. It's great for astral energy."

Louise, her eyes still closed, wondered if madness might be catching. Perhaps in heat it spread like mold.

But she must pull herself together. She opened her eyes and faced Sue Ellen.

"Tell me," she said, "just what experience you've had in caring for the elderly?"

"None," said Sue Ellen. "But I figure I can learn." And she smiled at Louise, who did not smile back.

"If I'm not mistaken," said Louise, "the ad you answered specifically asked for a 'well-qualified' companion?"

"'Well-qualified, CHEERFUL companion,'" said Sue Ellen, pulling the crumpled ad from her skirt pocket, "and I figured I was cheerful enough to make up for not being qualified." She kept on smiling to show Louise just how cheerful she was, though it was clear that Louise didn't like her one little bit. It made her sad. "I get along with almost everyone," she said, not wanting to boast, but it was true.

"The job is difficult," said Louise. "As you can see, he's not well. He'll need help walking, dressing, eating. In fact with *all* his personal needs."

"Peeing," said Eliot, afraid he'd been forgotten. And he liked shocking people, especially Louise.

Sue Ellen laughed. Louise did not. "Frankly," she said to Sue Ellen, "I have difficulty understanding why you applied."

"It's a long story," said Sue Ellen, not sure what she could say that Louise would understand. A Virgo, for sure, but one gone sour like fruit left too long on a tree. Sue Ellen felt for her with that pinched white face and bony hands. "The cold," she said at last, "it got to me.

I've been up north for fifteen years, and suddenly I felt the cold. Inside." She poked her chest and shook her head. "I'm twenty-nine."

Twenty-nine! Louise was fifty-one and felt a migraine coming on. An outrage to waste youth on someone like Sue Ellen. Louise doubted she'd even finished school.

"That does not answer my question," Louise said.

"Roots," said Sue Ellen. "I grew up down here." She saw Louise's eyes widen, and she laughed. "Not Palm Beach," she said. "Inland. My grandpa raised me and I figured I'd surprise him. Like I said, it's been fifteen years and we'd lost touch. Trouble is," she said, taking a deep breath, "turns out I was the one to be surprised. When I got in this morning, I called from the airport, and Georgie, our neighbor, told me he'd died two years ago. He died and I never even knew." Pulling a soiled Kleenex from her pocket, she blew her nose; quickly, Louise looked the other way. "It wasn't that we were close, you know, but I kept hoping. . . . Well, anyway, there I was with a one-way ticket to nowhere. So I bought a local paper, and sat down to think, and then I saw the ad, and here I am." She tried another cheerful smile, which was hard because truth to tell she wasn't feeling very cheerful, and anyway she could tell Louise wasn't liking her any better than before. So she stared at the pink foxes leaping all over Louise's high-necked dress and wondered why anyone would wear something so ugly, especially when that somebody had red hair.

Louise wondered if perhaps Sue Ellen had spent some time in a mental institution. "It is the money?" she asked. "Do you need money?"

Sue Ellen blinked. "Excuse me?" she said with what sounded like genuine surprise.

But who could tell. There was a certain softness to her face that reminded Louise of a woman she'd seen years ago, leaning against a derelict building at Broadway and 89th. Louise, who as always had her camera with her, had tried but could not bring herself to photograph the woman's face. It was somehow too intimate, too exposed. Though it was winter, the woman's feet were bare, her white toes striking against the winter rubble of a city street. She photographed the feet instead. Entitled *Survivor,* the photograph had been Louise's first success.

Louise sighed. "But why *this* job?" she said, trying one last time.

"Karma," said Sue Ellen. "And I liked the word 'companion.' It sounded cozy." She smiled at Louise, a shy smile, like a child's. "I get lonesome sometimes," she said.

Karma, thought Louise. Whatever next. She looked down at her father. He was so still. Perhaps he'd died. But she saw the sheet fluttering with his breath. How much more, she wondered, could she take? Of all the applicants, Sue Ellen was the only one he had approved. "You're the seventh," she said, more to herself than to Sue Ellen.

Sue Ellen clapped her hands. "I knew it!" she said. "My lucky number." When Louise stared at her, she smiled. "I'm Cancer," she said. "The seventh month."

"I see," Louise said, seeing nothing, wishing only for the strength to send her away.

"Actually," said Sue Ellen, "I'm really into it. Astrology, I mean. When in doubt, check it out. That's my motto, always has been. That's why I bought the paper today, to read my horoscope. And what do you think it was?"

"I have no idea," said Louise.

"USE CARE IN MOTION," said Sue Ellen. "So that's exactly what I did. I never read the paper carefully, but today I turned every page really slow, and read them top to bottom, and that's how come I saw the ad. I never would have otherwise."

She smiled at Louise as if she thought she'd won her over.

"I'm sorry," Louise said.

Eliot stirred, sensing danger in the air. "I sink," he said, "into oblivion." He chuckled, enjoying his joke. His voice came muffled as his head slipped from the pillow, his face half buried by the sheet.

He felt hands tugging, pulling him up. Louise pinched, her fingers bony, but Sue Ellen's hands were firm and plump, juices running beneath the skin.

"When can you start?" he asked.

"Right now," Sue Ellen said. "I travel light." She smiled at Louise to let her know she wanted to be friends. "If it's okay with your daughter, I mean."

"Of course it is," Eliot said. Hadn't he made his wishes clear? "Tell Esther to set for three."

Decisions tired him. He slept.

Louise looked down and watched him sleeping. His eyelids fluttered. What she would give to sleep like that! He slept as a child sleeps, palms up, his fingers curled. She thought of taking his picture now. Whenever she tried, he'd sulk and fidget. "You know I can't see," he'd say when Louise had come to visit, bringing her photographs to show him. "Can't see a thing," he'd said, long before his eyesight failed.

Over the years she'd tried to capture him on film, preserve some likeness. But always the light was too bright, the shade too deep; he would never sit still. And now at last it was too late. He lay on his back, his mouth open, his eyes closed, looking like someone she'd never seen before.

She looked at the photograph above his bed. It had always been her favorite, one taken by her mother on the beach when Louise was sixteen and dancing in her father's arms. The tide was out, the sand hard and smooth, and Eliot, in evening dress, black tails flying, was pointing his hand toward the sky. "The first star" is what he'd said. "Venus." And Louise remembered how he'd smiled, how he'd bent and kissed her cheek.

He had always been a ladies' man.

Now he slept. Louise turned, and pressed her forehead against the window. The glass was warm. The hot sun beat against the orange trees bent low with fruit, and on the terrace lizards lay, tongues flickering like fire.

"I think he likes me," Sue Ellen said, shyly, hoping to make her feel better.

"My father," said Louise, "likes no one but himself." The words once out immediately regretted. Such things were never said. She turned, frowning, to Sue Ellen.

"He is a gentleman," she said. "He must be treated with respect."

Sue Ellen's eyes were wide and puzzled. "Why!" She stretched her hand toward Louise. "I wouldn't dream. . . ."

But Eliot dreamt. On a white horse he rode across wet sand toward the enemy, clustered like coconuts beneath the bougainvillea. His saber raised, the rebel flag snapping above his head. "Charge!" he cried.

And hands lifted him, tied his robe, wheeled him into lunch. He smelled blossoms; he smelled soup. "Ah," he said. He smacked his lips. "Delicious." The warmth was delicious, sliding down inside. A gentle warmth. Clear soup was essential. He felt his strength returning. "Remember, my dear," he said. "For perfect bouillon you must always crack the bones."

"Okay, Mr. Jarvis."

Sue Ellen had already finished her soup. She certainly hoped there was more to come. In the heat she felt her appetite returning. She liked things sweet and thick, oatmeal with cream, stews and puddings. She'd rather not think of cracking bones.

But Mr. Jarvis was a gentleman all right. He had beautiful hands and elegant feet. Old as he was, his voice was full, like velvet, she thought. "Are you English?" she asked.

Eliot chuckled. He felt quite full, quite restored. His spoon held to his heart, he chanted, "'Into the valley of death rode the six hundred.'" He chuckled. "Does that answer you, my dear?"

"No," Sue Ellen said. Her stomach growled, and she coughed to cover the sound.

Coughing, she didn't cover her mouth. Louise saw white teeth and a small pink tongue. She looked away, at family portraits on the wall. Sunlight, filtered through the bamboo shutters, lay strips of shadows that looked like bars.

"The answer," said Louise, "is yes. On both sides. Both sides, in fact, came over on the Mayflower."

"Pilgrims!" said Sue Ellen. "Far out!"

"Confederates, my dear," said Eliot. "Five generations. Louise here is the last."

Sue Ellen reached out to pat his hand. His skin, though wrinkled, was very soft. He smelled of talcum. "But the South's going to rise again. Isn't that right?"

"Precisely," said Eliot. "Beauregard, though a relative, was a fool. I will show you my strategy after lunch."

Louise let her spoon drop to her plate.

"My father," she said, "lives in the past."

Sue Ellen smiled.

"I guess we all do, one way or another."

Louise saw a piece of parsley stuck between Sue Ellen's teeth.

"I wouldn't know," she said.

Eliot slapped the table. The soup bowls bounced. "Where's the roughage?" he said.

Perhaps they deserved each other, thought Louise. She rang the silver bell and waited. Waited, thinking of gold leaves dropping on the frozen ground, of bare branches pressed against a silver sky. As always, out of habit, she'd brought her camera down, but up north, negatives waited for release. Her life on hold.

The ringing made Sue Ellen jump. She picked the parsley from her teeth and waited to see what would happen next. Rich people were really something else. It was the kind of bell God might use to summon angels. In her white uniform, Esther might be an angel, or maybe a ghost. She was that quiet and that old. Older than Mr. Jarvis, with lips thin as hairpins and bumpy veins running up her skinny arms. She seemed to need the salad bowl for balance.

Sue Ellen was the last one served. She counted five pieces of lettuce, three cherry tomatoes, and one small egg. Maybe, she thought, rich people didn't have to eat. She was pretty sure that this was true when after the salad Esther brought in bowls of water, one for each. The bowls were small. Two gulps and it was gone. Not only that, but there was a hint of perfume in the taste. She couldn't help but grimace, though when Louise looked at her, she smiled. "Good," she said, not wanting Louise to think her rude.

Louise brought her hands up to her face. It was suddenly too much to bear. Her father blind, her mother dead. What friends she had were in New York. Who would believe what she'd just seen. She heard the ticking of the sideboard clock. The temperature was eighty-nine. Her father's age. She looked at him. He might die tomorrow or live for years.

Eliot bent above his finger bowl, his fingers dabbling. The water spilled. Drops lay on the polished table. He licked his fingers, one by one. He tasted flowers. He saw light shining in the drops of water. He saw it shimmering. "Lovely!" he said.

"Really," said Louise, "he should be in a home."

Eliot looked toward Louise. He saw shadow, nothing more.

"I am," he said. "My own."

Louise sighed. An only child, she'd had enough. "All right," she said. "We'll try it for a month. And then we'll see."

From New York she saw nothing, nothing at all. She slept better but not well enough, and when she slept she dreamt of spiders. Every night, her white phone cradled in her lap, she called.

"Marvelous!" her father said. "We appear to be ahead."

"Terrific!" said Sue Ellen, her voice juicy as though chewing gum. "We're having a real good time."

"I see," Louise said, but she saw nothing, could only imagine the two of them sitting side by side on the sun-porch sofa, their legs touching, the family portraits on the wall. Her mother had once spanked Louise for chewing gum. "Ladies do not!" is what she'd said. Sue Ellen, whatever she might be, was not a lady. Louise felt some relief that her mother had been spared this final humiliation. A true lady, she had died gracefully, slipping away in her eighty-first year. The day of the funeral a hurricane threatened. Rain beat against the windows; her father stayed home. "Devoted," guests murmured, and Louise had bowed her head. "Adored," she said, as if in prayer.

On Louise's dresser stood a photograph of her mother in bridal white, dress and train, and veil and gloves. Only her eyes were dark as, unsmiling, she stared at some point far beyond the camera. "What were you looking at?" Louise had asked her once. "Nothing," her mother said. "Nothing at all."

Sue Ellen, when Eliot napped after lunch, stripped and lay in the sun on the terrace. The terrace, ringed by a pink wall, was hot. Sweat poured from her skin, staining the bricks. Sue Ellen, eyes closed, smiled. The orange trees hung heavy with fruit, and squirrels chattered in the leaves. As the sun moved, Sue Ellen inched across the bricks. Thirsty, she plucked oranges, and biting through skin, she sucked the juice. With sticky fingers she planted the seeds.

At three she woke Eliot. "It's time," she said.

"For what?" asked Eliot, rising from a sea of sleep. He smelled oranges and gardenias.

"You'll see," said Sue Ellen, lifting him. "A surprise for your daughter when she comes back down."

"Louise has never liked surprises," Eliot said. Within the circle of Sue Ellen's arm, he sat upright on the bed.

"She'll like this one," Sue Ellen said.

Legs dangling, Eliot's feet felt cold. The floor seemed very far away. "I fell," said Eliot. "I lay there three hours before someone came."

Sue Ellen heard the quiver in his voice. "It won't happen again," she said. She held him close. Light as a leaf, she thought. His hand was clutching at her leg. Beneath his skin, she saw the delicate tracery of veins.

"We're going to get you walking," she said. "We're going to get you to that beach."

The beach was so close that on still days Sue Ellen heard waves rolling in. She liked the sound, like clapping hands. "Listen," she said, pulling his shirt down over his head. "You hear those waves?"

Eliot cocked his head to listen. "Break, break, break," is what he said.

The shirt on, Sue Ellen bent to button. "Nothing's going to break," she said, "but first we've got to get you walking fast enough to cross the highway between here and there."

"I'd rather not," said Eliot. "The enemy, you know."

"You don't want to yet," Sue Ellen said, "but I know you will. There's lots of time."

Time. Sue Ellen forgot to wind the clocks: the hands stopped moving. Sunlight woke them into morning, Esther called them into lunch. The days flowed, one into the next. Sue Ellen hid the wheelchair, and on her arm Eliot shuffled from room to room. His legs trembled and his heart fluttered like a bird's.

Each night he spent time talking to Louise.

"She's killing me. She wants me dead," said Eliot, chuckling.

Louise, phone pressed to her ear, watched snow drift against the window, slide down onto city streets. The day before she'd watched a car leap from the curb, and catching a baby's stroller under its wheels, tear away. The baby's mittens, tied to strings, had fluttered like blue butterflies. Watching, Louise felt no surprise. She stood beside the mother who didn't move, her arms outstretched, her fingers curled, and felt relief the baby wasn't hers. She saw the hands, cropped, framed by glass, a curve of agony against the black wet street.

She sighed. "I better come down."

"Nonsense," Eliot said. "I'm fine."

"Louise has always lacked a sense of humor," he said as Sue Ellen tucked him into bed. She smoothed the hair back from his forehead.

"She loves you," said Sue Ellen. "She just worries."

"She does not know what love is," said Eliot, crossly.

Sue Ellen wondered if that might be true. "Sleep tight," she said. She kissed his cheek.

The slow days tired her. She slept and woke and slept again, a rise and fall like riding waves. She smelled the jasmine, heard the rustle of the palms. The bed was soft. She heard the sound of Eliot's breathing coming through the intercom. She didn't mind; she liked the company. When she slept, she dreamt of love.

"There was this baby on the plane," she said at breakfast. Her face felt soft, her skin polished by the sun.

"I want my bran," said Eliot, and Sue Ellen rang the bell.

"This is the life," she said.

Sunlight filled the room, and on the table gardenias floated in a crystal bowl. Esther brought cereal and cream and toast and coffee. "Thank you," said Sue Ellen, smiling. She knew now not to drink her finger bowl. She poured cream on their cereal, into their coffee. "He was the cutest," she said. "I never knew babies could be that cute."

"How many have you had?" said Eliot, smacking his lips, enjoying the crunch.

Sue Ellen laughed. "None," she said. She tipped her bowl to swallow the cream. "I've never married."

"Good," said Eliot.

She was his. Her hands woke him in the morning, tucked him in at night. She filled his days. She was his days. He remembered his manners.

"Though not from want of suitors. Of that I'm sure."

He smiled at Sue Ellen, but she was looking at the flowers. Gardenias she'd picked yesterday; already they were turning brown. "I guess," she said. "But somehow I could never seem to settle down. I'm twenty-nine." She sighed. "Who would have thought?"

She didn't think. She watched the dust motes rise and drift. She watched them settle on books and chairs. She felt the weight of house, of history. "All these things," she said, "this stuff about your ancestors. Does it make you feel safe?"

Eliot straightened in his chair. "I have never lacked for courage," he said.

"I know," Sue Ellen said. She patted his hand. "You're something else."

He was. Every day he grew a little stronger. He learned to do buttons, to get to the bathroom by himself. All alone he fought his way across the living room from chair to chair. Grasping the piano, he flexed his legs. "Knee bends," he said, gasping. Sue Ellen heard his knees creak, but as for bending she couldn't see a thing.

"I am just so proud," she said. "Now let me see."

She took his hand and traced the lifeline on his palm.

"I thought so," she said. "It says here you're going to live forever."

Eliot chuckled. "I never doubted."

Exhausted, he felt the battle all but won.

He slept. Sue Ellen slept too, flat on her back in tropical sun. Her nose peeled pink. The orange seeds sprouted, tiny shoots too small to touch. She checked her palm and held her breath. Every day she read the paper; every day her horoscope said USE CARE IN MOTION, and in the heavens Venus was heading right for Mars.

She could only hope. She picked oranges and oleanders, filling the house with fruits and flowers.

Eliot woke to the roar of guns. "They're coming," he said. "We must prepare."

"The waves," Sue Ellen said. "The wind's blowing in from the ocean today."

"We must take no chances," Eliot said. Rising slowly, he shuffled to his desk. "Open it," he said, and Sue Ellen did. "What do you see?" he asked. Sue Ellen saw old photographs and rusty keys.

"Not much," she said.

Eliot took command. "Pull out the center drawer," he said. "Now slide your hand in. Feel the latch."

Sue Ellen slid her hand in, caught the latch. A secret drawer sprang open.

"Far out!" she said. Inside the drawer were stacks of bills, all tied in bundles. "But shouldn't you keep them in a bank?"

"Confederate," said Eliot. "My legacy. The South will rise again, you know."

"I know," Sue Ellen said. "But counterfeit money. I mean, shouldn't it look like the real thing?"

Eliot frowned. "I had thought you were on my side," he said.

"I am," Sue Ellen said. "As long as you don't try and use it. You'd get in trouble."

"The time will come," said Eliot.

He closed the drawer.

Afternoons they walked up and down the street, Eliot on Sue Ellen's arm. The street was sheltered. Only the tips of tall palms swayed in the wind. Across the highway they heard waves breaking on the beach. They crept along, Sue Ellen's face tipped up to catch the sun. They barely moved. Sue Ellen didn't mind.

Time stood still, and she was happy.

They ate ice cream for dessert. Esther served and Sue Ellen poured the chocolate sauce. Scraping Eliot's plate, she spooned the last of it into his mouth, clicking the spoon against his teeth. "They're mine," he said. The sweetness of the chocolate produced an ache.

"You're something else," Sue Ellen said. "I think it's time to hit that beach. You ready to try?"

"Not yet," said Eliot. "We are surrounded."

Louise called. "It's been a month," she said. "I'm coming down."

"No need for that," said Eliot. "I couldn't be in better hands."

Louise had noticed Sue Ellen's hands. The nails chewed down to the quick, the skin more gray than white. "Mother would not approve," she said.

"Your mother," he said, "is dead."

Louise's fingers tightened on the phone. "I'll talk to Sue Ellen, please," she said. Waiting, she heard the click and mumble of the phone being passed from hand to hand. On the wall her photographs hung framed. Winter branches against a winter sky. "The stark simplicity," the critics said. "A purity of vision." Louise sighed.

"I'm coming down," she said.

"Terrific!" said Sue Ellen. "You won't believe your eyes!"

Louise's eyes were not what they had been. She had to strain to see things at a distance. For reading she wore glasses. She was almost fifty-two.

"Tomorrow," she said. "In time for dinner. We need to talk."

Hanging up, Sue Ellen smiled. "She's going to be so pleased," she said.

"I have my doubts," said Eliot. "She was often peevish as a child."

They sat together on the sofa. The night was warm, the windows open. Sue Ellen thought of Venus; she thought of Mars.

"I guess I'm scared."

Eliot took her hand, holding it between his own. "We shall take the offensive."

"I think it's important to be nice," Sue Ellen said. "To make her feel welcome, you know."

"Precisely," Eliot said. "We'll plan a party."

"Far out," Sue Ellen said. "I love a party."

She spent the next day polishing silver. She waxed the wood, and standing on the table, washed the chandelier. The crystal tinkled, a sound so pretty Sue Ellen laughed out loud. She felt much better. This morning her horoscope had read PREPARE FOR CHANGE. She felt her psychic juices flowing.

Eliot ordered dinner, sent for wine, and rested. At seven he dressed with care, and at eight they waited together at the door.

Louise, weighted down by luggage, came slowly up the walk. She noticed that in moonlight Sue Ellen's face looked black. Her father stood there, leaning on Sue Ellen's arm. She kissed his cheek, but could not bring herself to shake Sue Ellen's hand. "I'm tired," she said. "The trip."

The house reeked of flowers, the stench of stagnant water, rotting leaves. "A homecoming dinner," said Sue Ellen. "Your father planned it just for you." She wore a necklace made of tiny shells. Her arms were bare. She touched Louise's shoulder. "Doesn't he look great?" Her skirt had tiny bells that jingled when she walked. Louise pulled away.

"I wouldn't know," she said, her voice so cold Sue Ellen shivered.

Eliot felt a sudden draft. Alert, he cocked his head and listened. "As I thought. A night attack."

"Let's eat first," Sue Ellen said. "We'll need our strength." A full moon always made her hungry. It made her nervous too. Born on the cusp, she was especially sensitive to the moon. She drew the curtains in the dining room.

"There," she said. "We're safe till morning."

The curtains drawn, the room was stifling. Louise found it hard to breathe. The soup was hot; the spoon was too. She dropped it with a clatter. Eliot jumped.

"I have my doubts," he said, soup dribbling down his chin.

Louise closed her eyes to block him out. Up north, she thought, the snow was falling, cold and quiet. Only this afternoon she'd looked out the window of the plane as it was gliding down the runway to see the wing was coated with ice. She'd held her breath as the plane lifted through the snow, groaning with the extra weight. She'd waited, imagining any minute the creak of metal, break of bone.

It was not death she minded, but the fall.

"I'm tired," she said. "We almost crashed."

Eliot's soup was gone. Licking his spoon, he waved it in the air. Once he had fallen, watching, surprised, as the floor rose up to meet his face. He smiled at his dinner guests.

"United we stand," he said.

"We are united," said Sue Ellen, smiling across the table at Louise. "We waited for you. Tomorrow we're walking to the beach."

"You shouldn't humor him."

"I'm not," Sue Ellen said, surprised. "I'll bet he can make it now."

"Not that. His mind. The Civil War."

"It's just his way. Underneath I think he knows."

Knows what? What had her father ever known? The candles flickered; the table gleamed. She might be a child again, white socks and tightly braided hair, called in to greet the guests. "Curtsy now," her mother said, and Louise bobbed, pressing damp fingers into white-gloved hands. "Who's this?" her father had said, eyebrows raised in mock surprise. He'd laughed, enjoying his joke. The other guests were laughing too, while Louise hid blushing behind her hands. Only her mother sat, unsmiling. "Up straight, Louise. One always makes an effort."

All her life. An effort. She pushed her soup away. "Mother," she said, looking at Sue Ellen, "was a true lady."

"I'm sure she was," Sue Ellen said, wishing Louise would eat her soup so she could ring. The soup was thin, Sue Ellen hungry.

"They were devoted to each other."

"Cold," said Eliot. "Cold as ice."

Sue Ellen patted him on the shoulder. "You'll warm up soon," she said, and decided to go ahead and ring. She rang it loud. Eliot chuckled.

"The call to arms," he said.

Louise looked at her mother's bell in Sue Ellen's hand. The nails still chewed, the knuckles raw, cheap silver bracelets on her wrists.

"This can't go on," she said. She felt relief. A lifting.

Sue Ellen heard the joyful anger in Louise's voice. Carefully she set the bell down on the table. "I was thinking," she said, "maybe we could take a picnic, the three of us. A picnic would be real nice, especially if the wind stops blowing."

"Out of the question," Louise said, but a bit more gently than before. She had family on her side, and could afford to be more charitable. Besides, she heard the longing in Sue Ellen's voice, a child's longing, small and sad.

"What you need," she said, "is family of your own. You're young and there's still time."

"It feels like time's the one thing I haven't got." She stared into the candle flame. "I'm twenty-nine," she said.

Her breath touched the flame and set it dancing. Eliot watched, entranced as the light spun circles. He stretched his hand toward it; he couldn't reach.

"Time is of the essence," he said.

"I know that," said Sue Ellen, "but it's hard. All my life I've been a rolling stone, and what do I have to show for it?"

She lifted her hands. Eliot heard the bracelets jingle. Reaching out, he caught her hand and brought it to his lips. The skin was hot.

"The money," he said, "is yours."

Louise went stiff. "The money is mother's."

Sue Ellen smiled and shook her head. "You're real kind," she said. "A real gentleman. But I don't know what I'd do with it."

"Why use it, of course," said Eliot. "Your wish is my command."

He released her hand and waited. Sue Ellen stared into the candle flame. She liked the way the light spread so the whole room fell away.

"I guess I haven't gotten much farther than the beach in the wish department. Mostly I take things a day at a time."

"Tomorrow," said Louise. "Tomorrow you will have to go."

But Sue Ellen kept right on staring at the flame.

"Once," she said, "when I was real little, Grandpa took me to the beach. Just once. I'd begged and begged. 'Little Mary Sunshine' he used to call me. Didn't mean it as a compliment though. He took life real hard." Sue Ellen sighed. "Well, the minute we got there, he started in to dig this hole. He didn't bring a spade or anything, just his hands, but the sand was soft. He dug like a dog, you know, bending down and scooping it out between his legs. I just stood there watching, thinking he was playing. Maybe he was. I'd never seen him play before. When he was done, he straightened up, groaning, holding onto his back and all. 'Get in,' he said. His face was all red. Anyway, I thought it was a game, so I did. I got in, and right away he started shoveling the sand back into the hole until the only part of me left showing was my head. I couldn't move, not even a toe. I couldn't even move my neck, but I knew he was standing there. I heard his breathing. He was breathing real hard. 'Let me out,' I said. He didn't though.

"'Now you know what life feels like,' he said. 'Now you know.'"

Louise felt a shivering inside.

"Well," said Sue Ellen, "I guess I did, and I didn't like it one little bit. Sometimes I think I've been running ever since. Sometimes. . . ." She leaned toward Louise. "Sometimes I just get so scared!"

Louise's shivering increased. She couldn't understand it. Perhaps she was coming down with something even though she'd just arrived. She felt a cold wind blowing through her.

Eliot slapped the table hard. "Time to plan a counterattack."

Sue Ellen was embarrassed. She gave herself a shake. "I don't know what got into me," she said. "Going on like that."

She looked at Louise across the table.

"It's not your fault."

As if Louise might think it was.

During the night it rained, a steady drumming on the roof. Eliot, sleeping, heard horses galloping as he danced on the beach, his daughter in his arms. Light as a cloud in silver slippers and a dusting of freckles on her nose. "Daddy," she said. "Daddy." Smiling into his eyes as the horses drew nearer, and he was not prepared. "Darling," he cried. But no one answered. No one came.

Sue Ellen woke to the sound of rain. The room was dark, the moon behind the clouds. Her body made a hollow in the bed. She hugged the warmth, listened to the lacy rustle of wet leaves, the water falling from the roof. Out there, her tiny trees were cupped like hands to catch the rain. They were so small, no bigger than her little finger. She hoped they would survive without her.

Louise slept soundly. She dreamt of sand. She dreamt of flying, the plane's slow lifting, lumbering up through heavy cloud.

She woke, remembering the dazzle of sudden sunlight on the wing, the instant shattering of the ice.

She woke refreshed, not knowing why. The rain had stopped, the morning blue and cool, as if some balance had been restored.

Rising, she saw Sue Ellen's door was open, her father's closed. The house was quiet, the sun just rising. Over the ocean, the sky was pink.

She slipped outside, her camera slung across her shoulder, and walked toward the ocean. The street was still. She saw crushed shells embedded in cement. She thought about Sue Ellen's story. There were no cars in sight. Crossing the highway, she eased through the private gate up to a small rise of grass to where the beach began.

And there she stopped.

Below, by the water's edge, her father stood, leaning on two canes, and dressed to kill in white ducks and a dark blue blazer. The sea was a shield of burnished gold, and on white sand Sue Ellen danced, her hands flung up toward the sky.

Louise heard bells jingling on her skirt. She saw brown legs and pink soles flashing as Sue Ellen spun her way, and stopped. She heard her laugh, a high bright sound.

"We made it!" Sue Ellen cried. "Come on down!"

Louise saw her father turn to look. "Louise," she heard Sue Ellen say.

Louise saw her father smile and lift one cane slowly in the air.

"We've won, my dear."

Lifting the cane, he held it, a sword, a beacon above his head as Louise brought her camera into focus, and snapping the shutter, heard the click.

ILLINOIS SHORT FICTION

Crossings by Stephen Minot
A Season for Unnatural Causes by Philip F. O'Connor
Curving Road by John Stewart
Such Waltzing Was Not Easy by Gordon Weaver

Rolling All the Time by James Ballard
Love in the Winter by Daniel Curley
To Byzantium by Andrew Fetler
Small Moments by Nancy Huddleston Packer

One More River by Lester Goldberg
The Tennis Player by Kent Nelson
A Horse of Another Color by Carolyn Osborn
The Pleasures of Manhood by Robley Wilson, Jr.

The New World by Russell Banks
The Actes and Monuments by John William Corrington
Virginia Reels by William Hoffman
Up Where I Used to Live by Max Schott

The Return of Service by Jonathan Baumbach
On the Edge of the Desert by Gladys Swan
Surviving Adverse Seasons by Barry Targan
The Gasoline Wars by Jean Thompson

Desirable Aliens by John Bovey
Naming Things by H. E. Francis
Transports and Disgraces by Robert Henson
The Calling by Mary Gray Hughes

Into the Wind by Robert Henderson
Breaking and Entering by Peter Makuck
The Four Corners of the House by Abraham Rothberg
Ladies Who Knit for a Living by Anthony E. Stockanes

Pastorale by Susan Engberg
Home Fires by David Long
The Canyons of Grace by Levi Peterson
Babaru by B. Wongar

Bodies of the Rich by John J. Clayton
Music Lesson by Martha Lacy Hall
Fetching the Dead by Scott R. Sanders
Some of the Things I Did Not Do by Janet Beeler Shaw

Honeymoon by Merrill Joan Gerber
Tentacles of Unreason by Joan Givner
The Christmas Wife by Helen Norris
Getting to Know the Weather by Pamela Painter

Birds Landing by Ernest Finney
Serious Trouble by Paul Friedman
Tigers in the Wood by Rebecca Kavaler
The Greek Generals Talk by Phillip Parotti

Singing on the Titanic by Perry Glasser
Legacies by Nancy Potter
Beyond This Bitter Air by Sarah Rossiter
Scenes from the Homefront by Sara Vogan